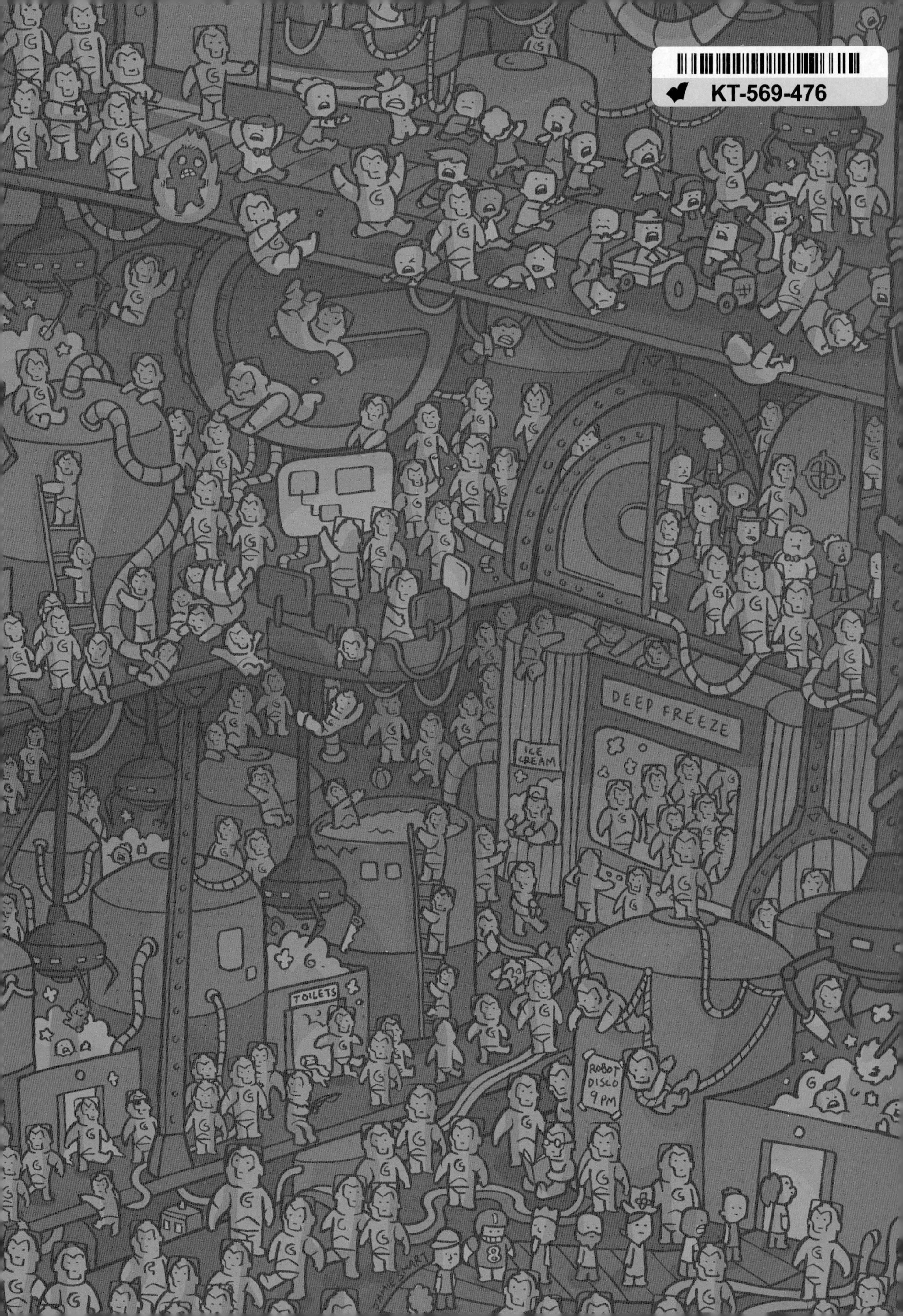
DEEP FREEZE
ICE CREAM
TOILETS
ROBOT DISCO 9PM

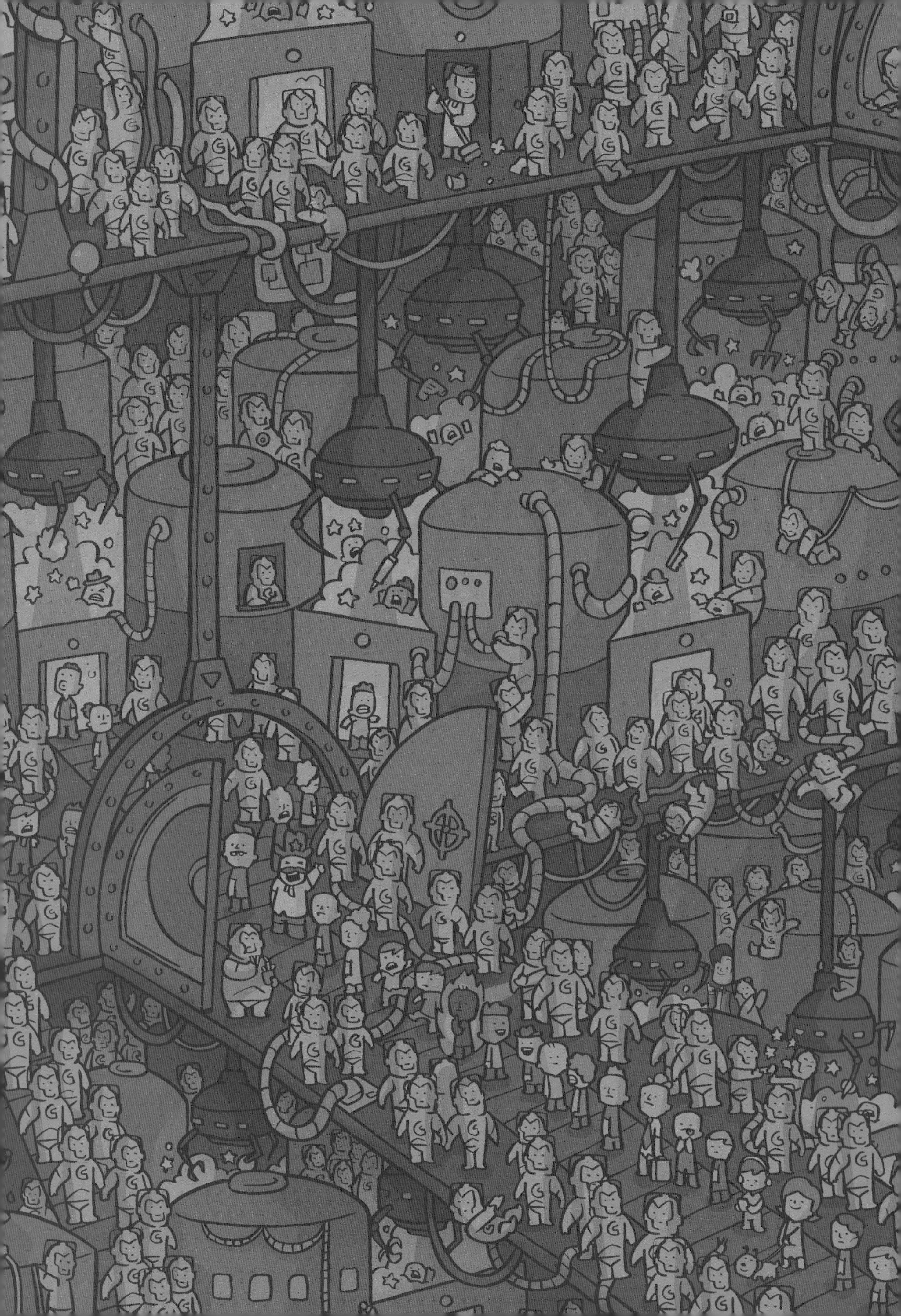

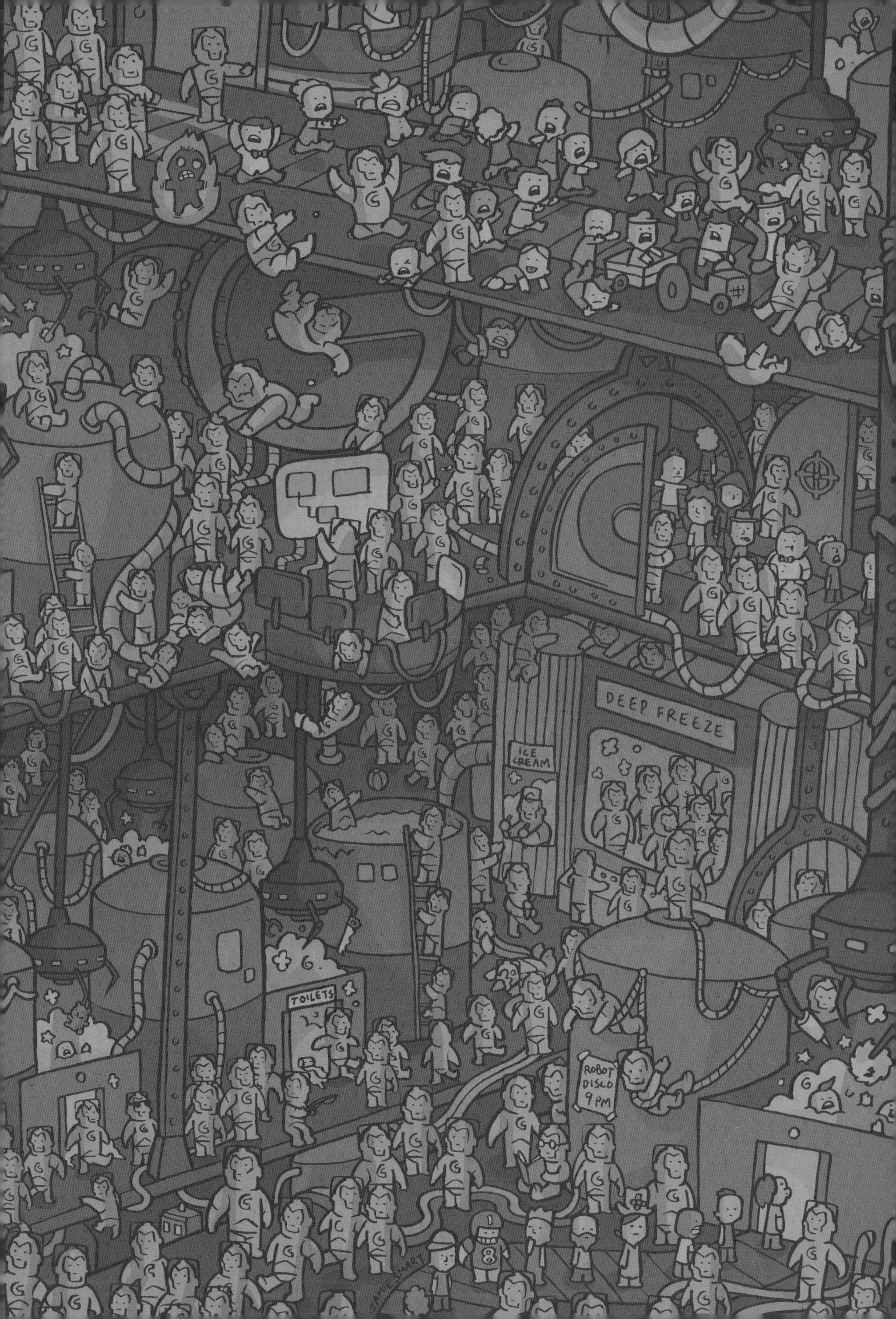
DEEP FREEZE
ICE CREAM
TOILETS
ROBOT DISCO 9PM

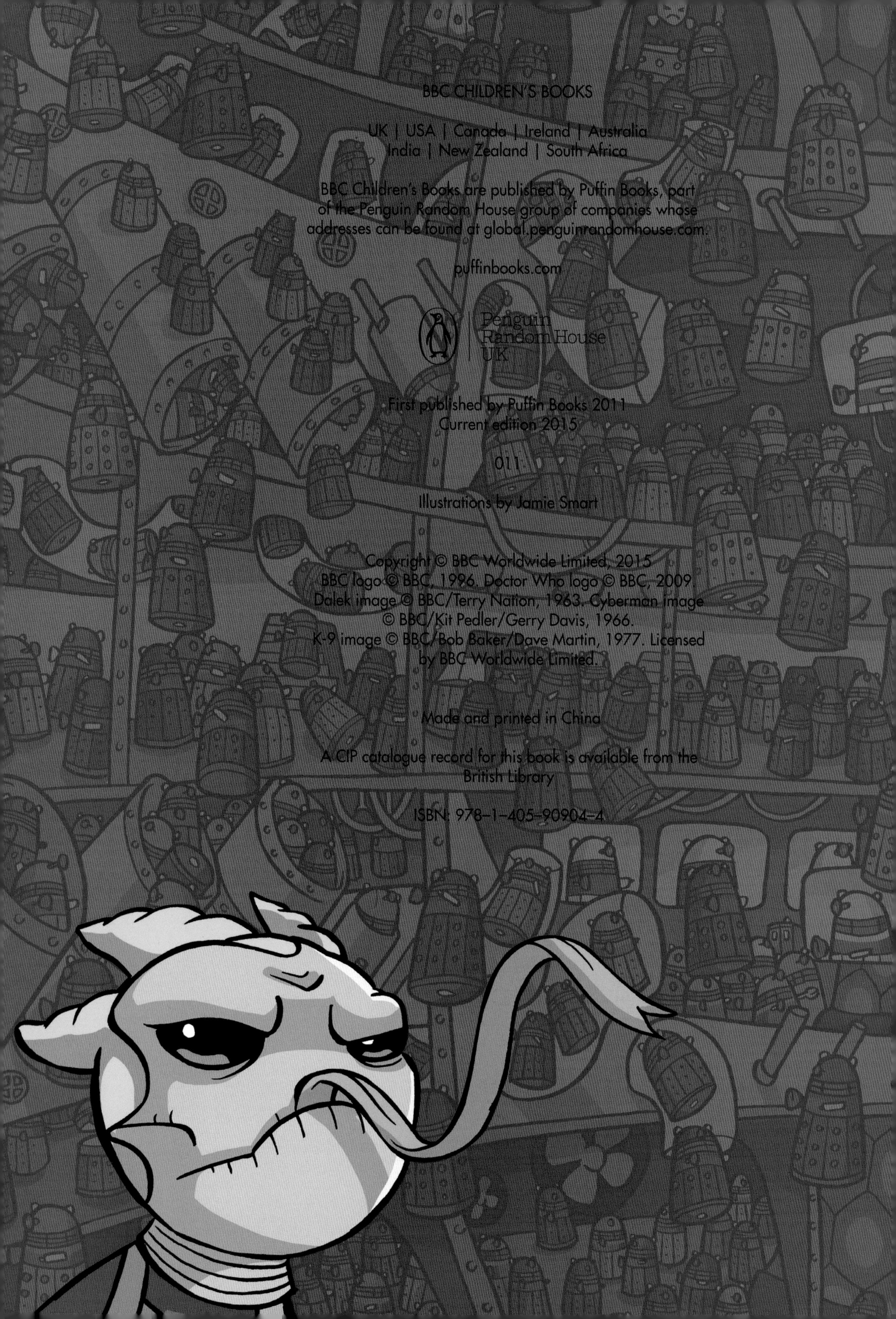

BBC CHILDREN'S BOOKS

UK | USA | Canada | Ireland | Australia
India | New Zealand | South Africa

BBC Children's Books are published by Puffin Books, part of the Penguin Random House group of companies whose addresses can be found at global.penguinrandomhouse.com.

puffinbooks.com

Penguin Random House UK

First published by Puffin Books 2011
Current edition 2015

011

Illustrations by Jamie Smart

Made and printed in China

A CIP catalogue record for this book is available from the British Library

ISBN: 978–1–405–90904–4

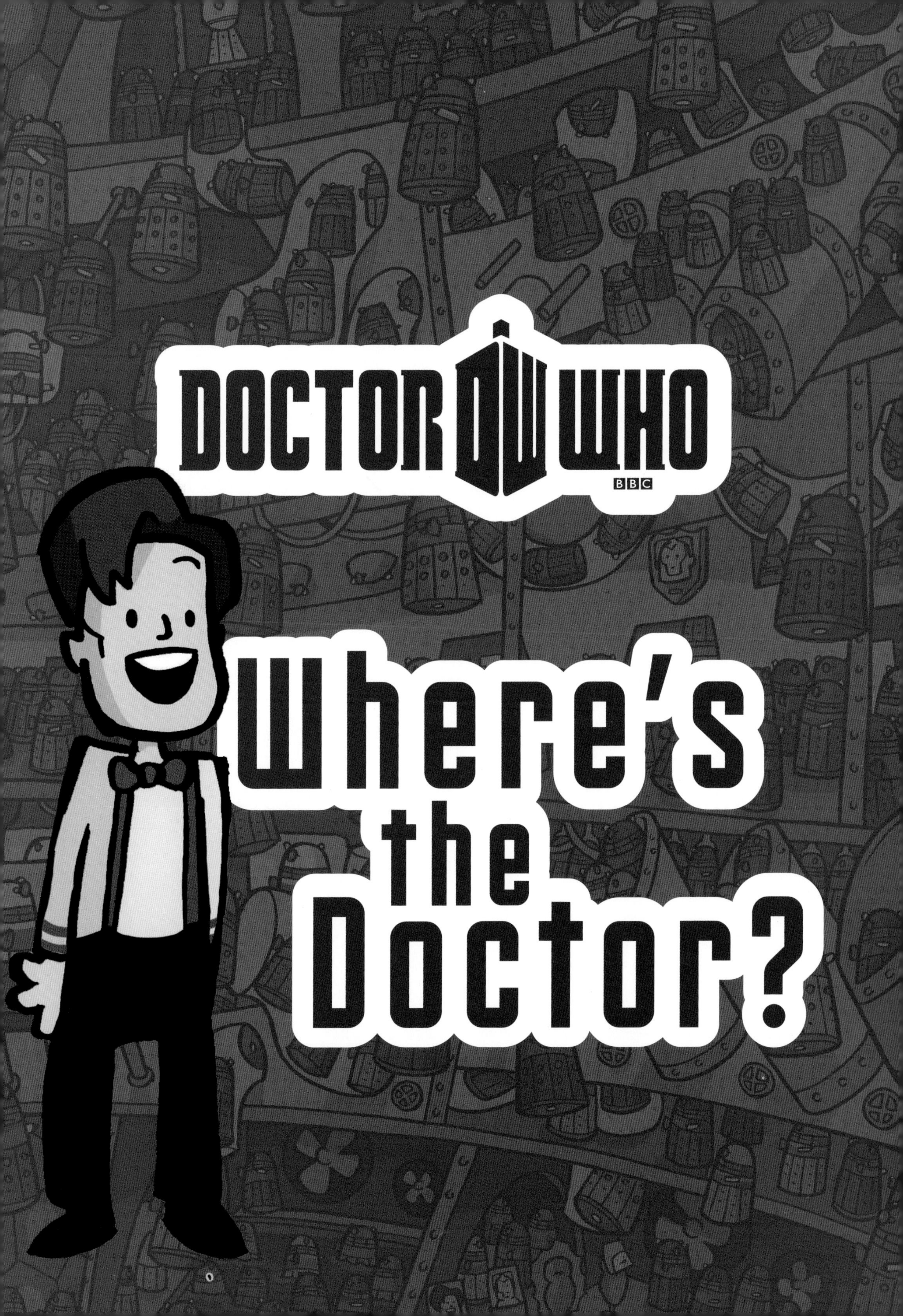

DOCTOR WHO

BBC

Where's the Doctor?

Contents

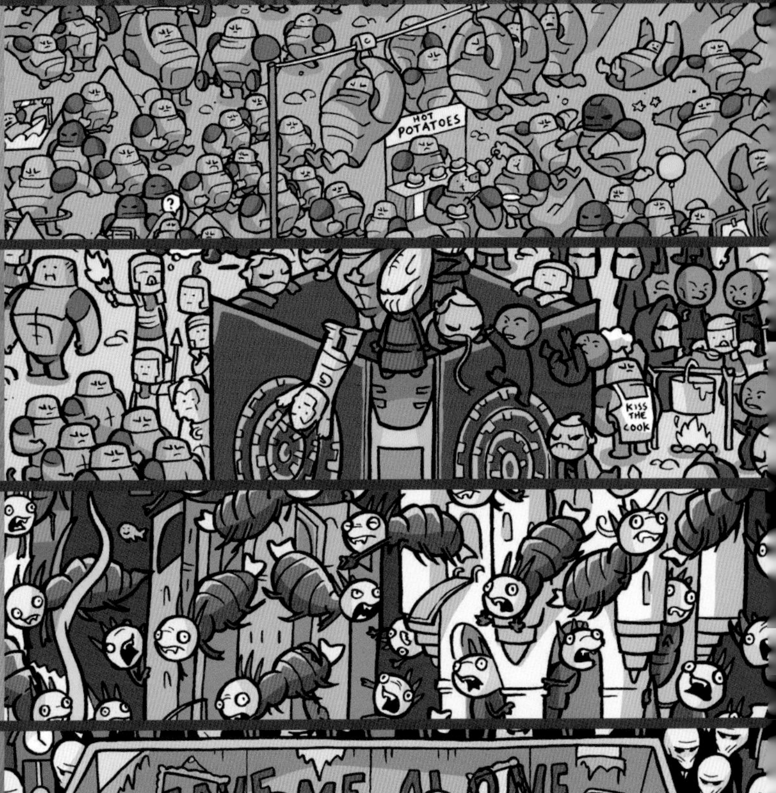

HOT POTATOES
KISS THE COOK
LEAVE ME ALONE

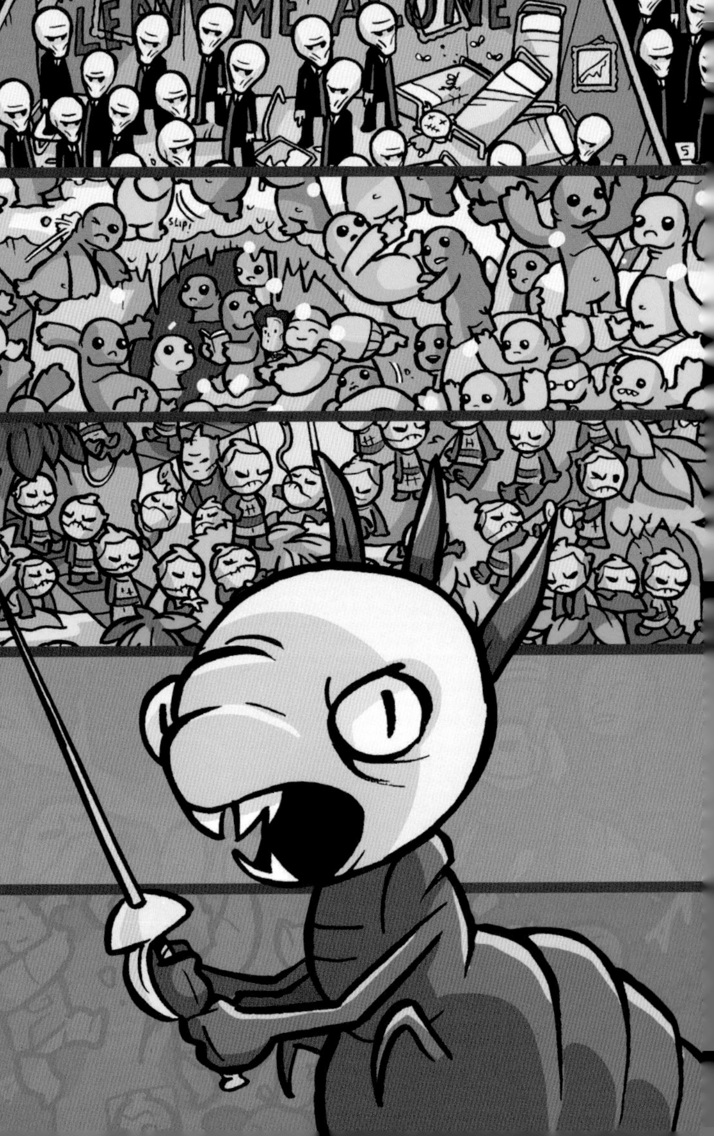

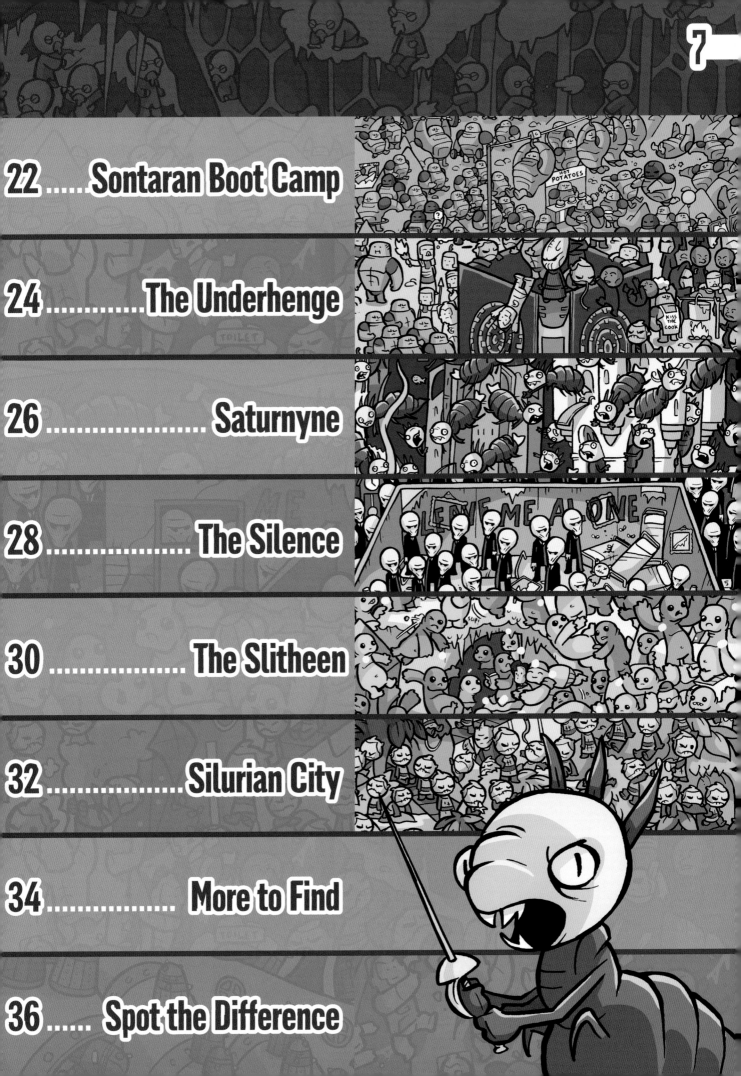

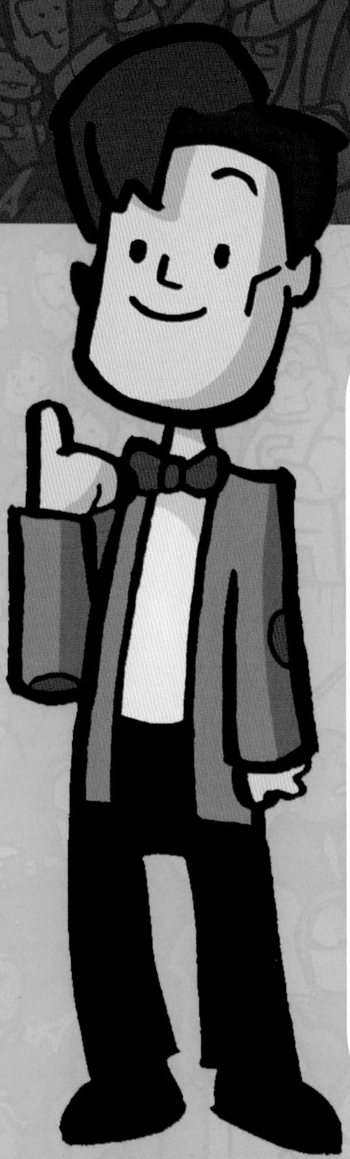

Where *is* the Doctor?

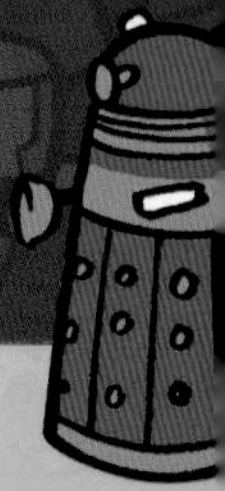

The Doctor is an intergalactic man of mystery, travelling through time and space, never knowing where he will end up from one day to the next. His faithful ship and oldest friend, the TARDIS, takes him wherever he needs to go – sometimes the Doctor can control the destination, but more often the TARDIS decides and transports him to wherever he is needed most.

Many have tried to find the Doctor, from human organisations like L.I.N.D.A and Torchwood, to the Shadow Proclamation and all manner of alien enemies who want to destroy the Time Lord. They've followed his progress over hundreds of years, tracking him around the world and across the galaxies.

Spotter's List

The following things can be found in every scene:

The Doctor

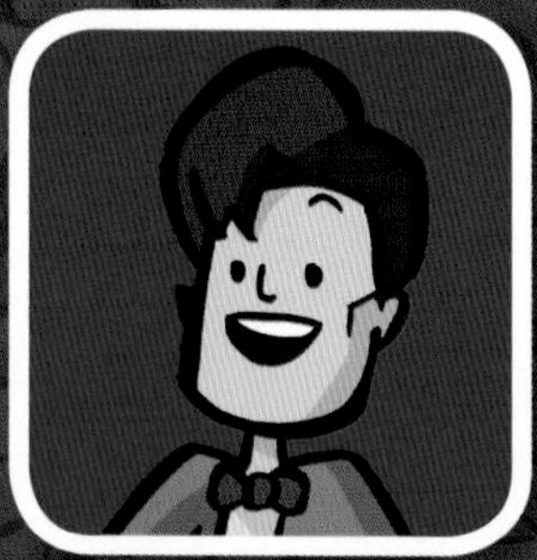

The TARDIS

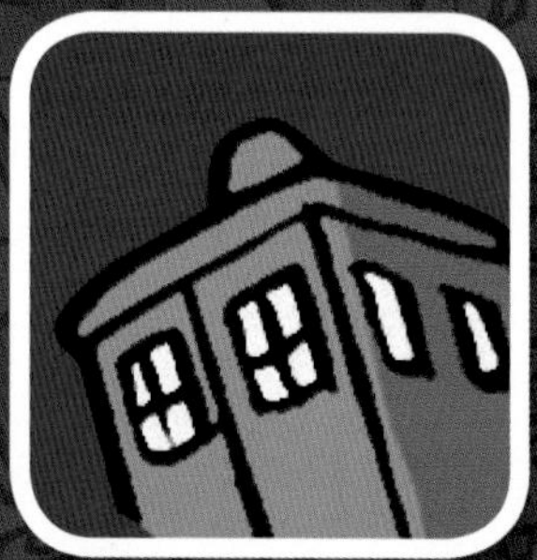

Amy Pond

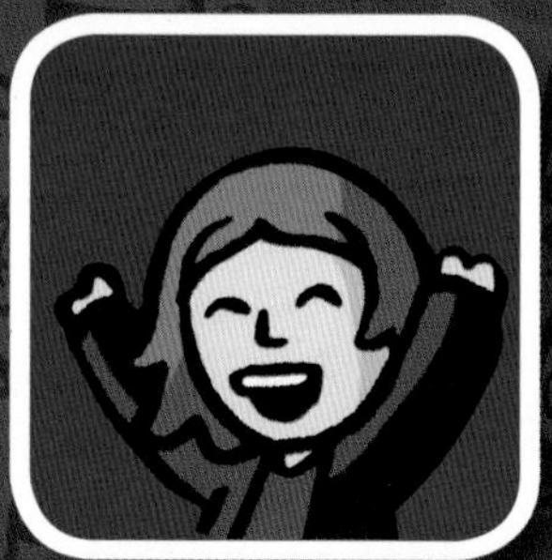

Rory Williams

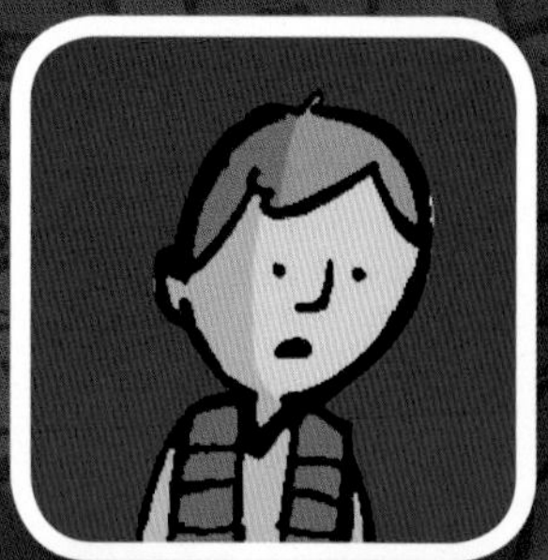

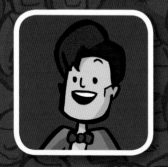

Some have even laid traps for him and, at times, have been successful in catching him. But there's one thing you must never do, and that is put the Doctor in a trap. The Doctor won't be held for long and always escapes to fight another day, continuing on his endless journey through the stars.

Enclosed in these pages are just a few of the places the Doctor has visited. Amy Pond and Rory Williams are hiding here with him, along with his TARDIS. There are also many other things to search for on page 34.

Can you succeed where many have failed and find them?

Tricky Spotter's List

The following things can be found somewhere in the book:

Fido the Dog   **Fido's dinner**   **Fido's Ball**

Judoon on the Moon

There are many Judoon upon the moon, but where's the Doctor?

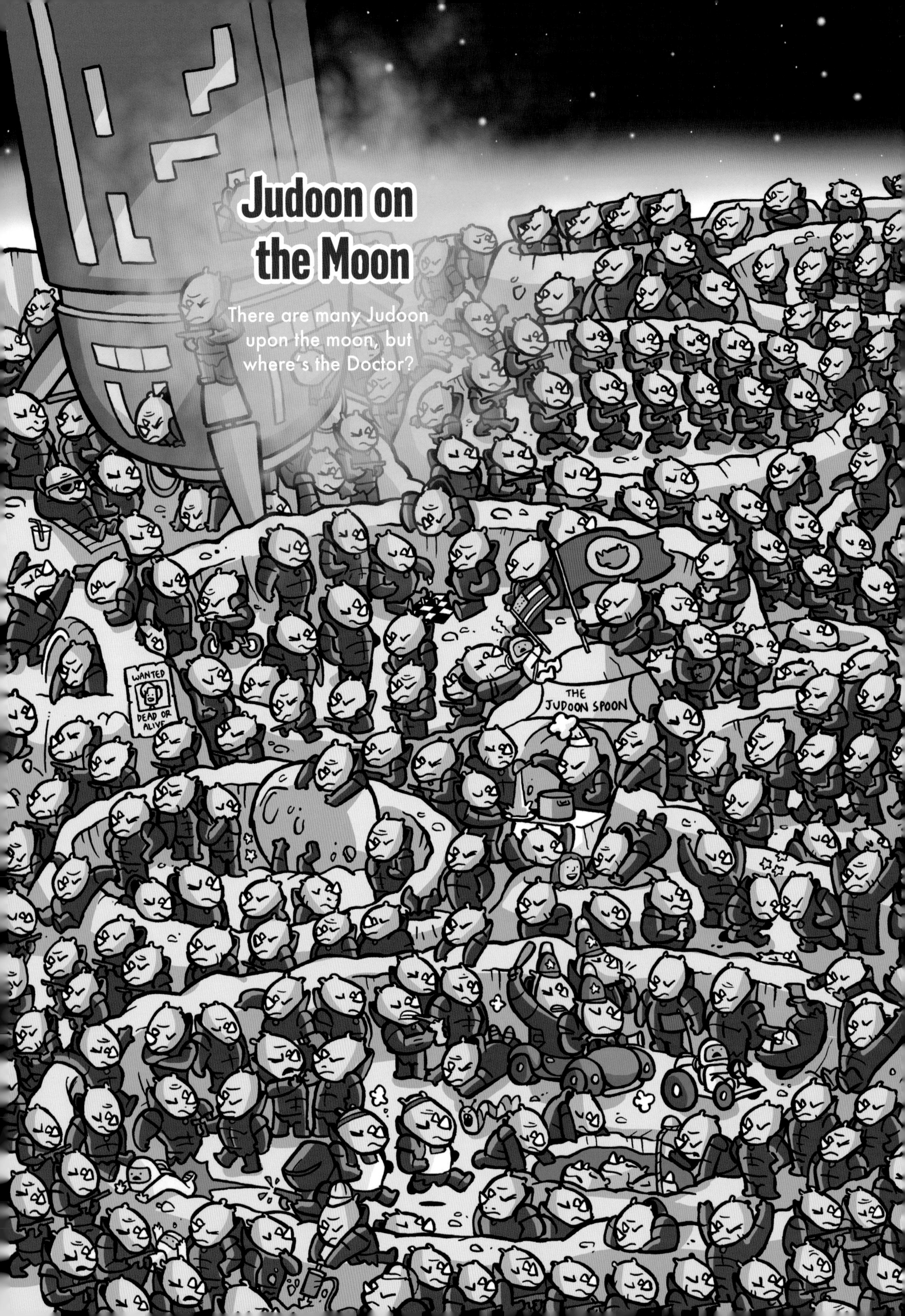
WANTED
DEAD OR ALIVE
THE JUDOON SPOON

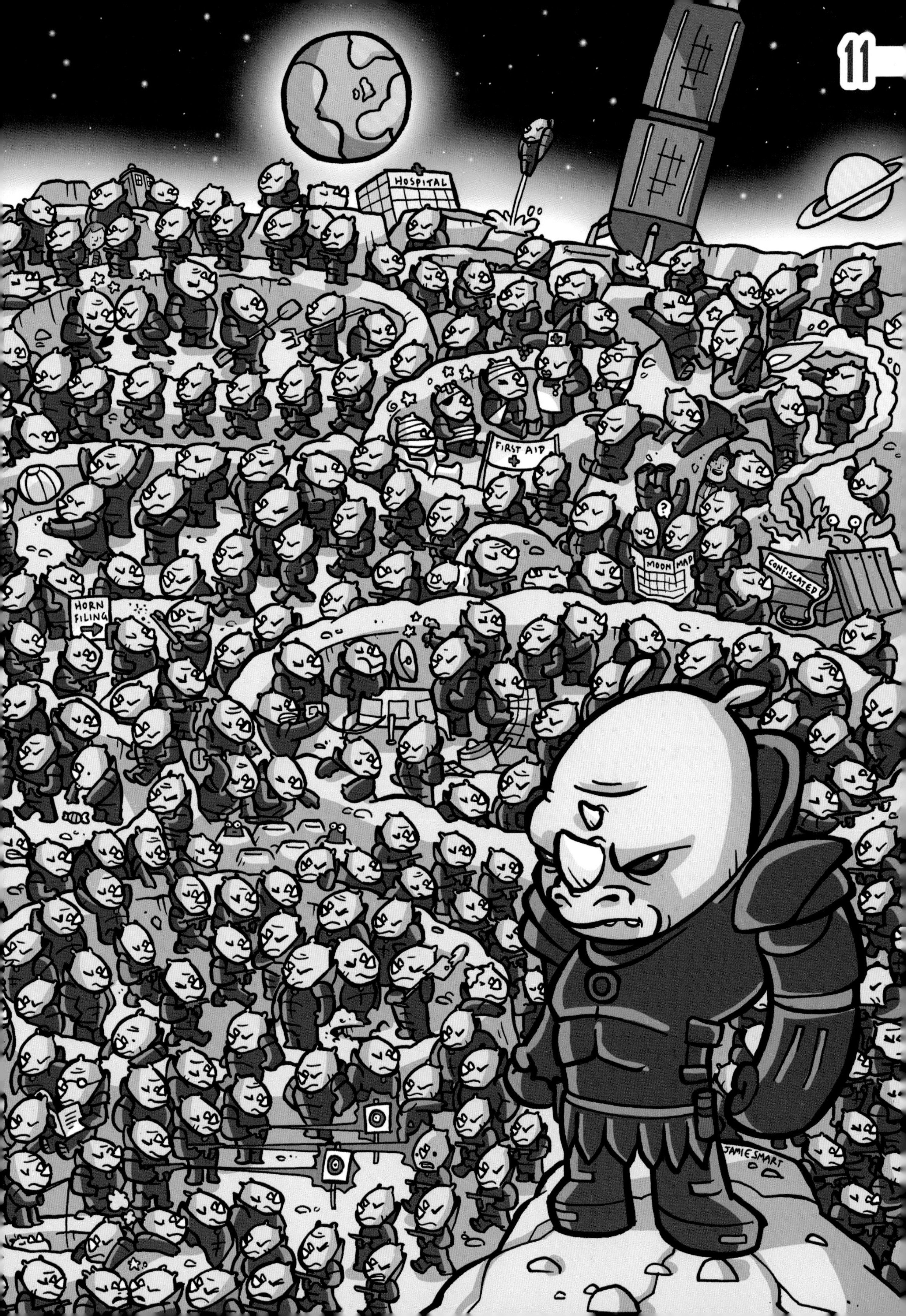
HOSPITAL
FIRST AID
MOON MAP
CONFISCATED
HORN FILING
JAMIE SMART

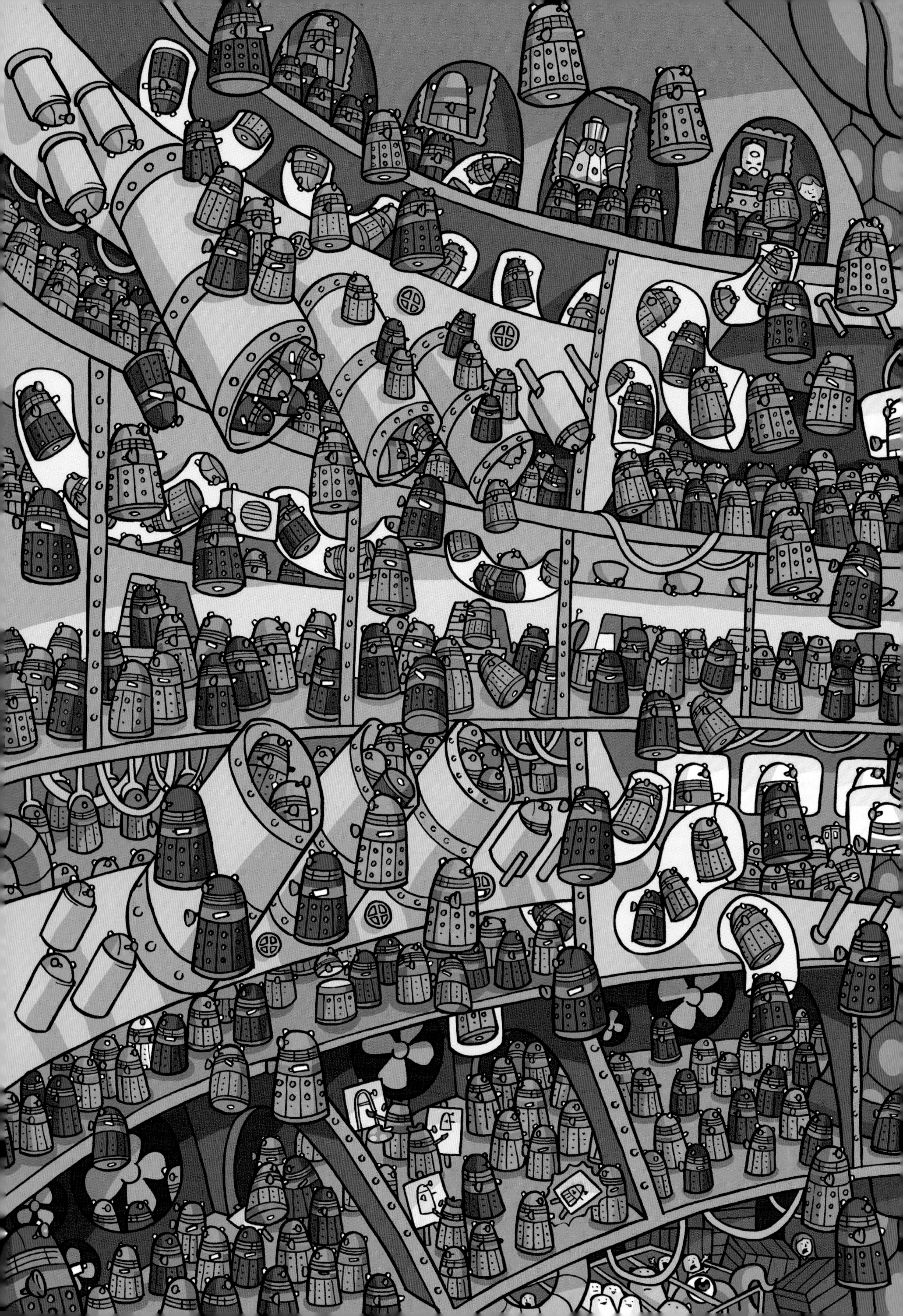

Dalek Ship

A ship packed with Daleks is a very dangerous place for the Doctor and Amy Pond to be hanging out! Can you spot him before they exterminate him?

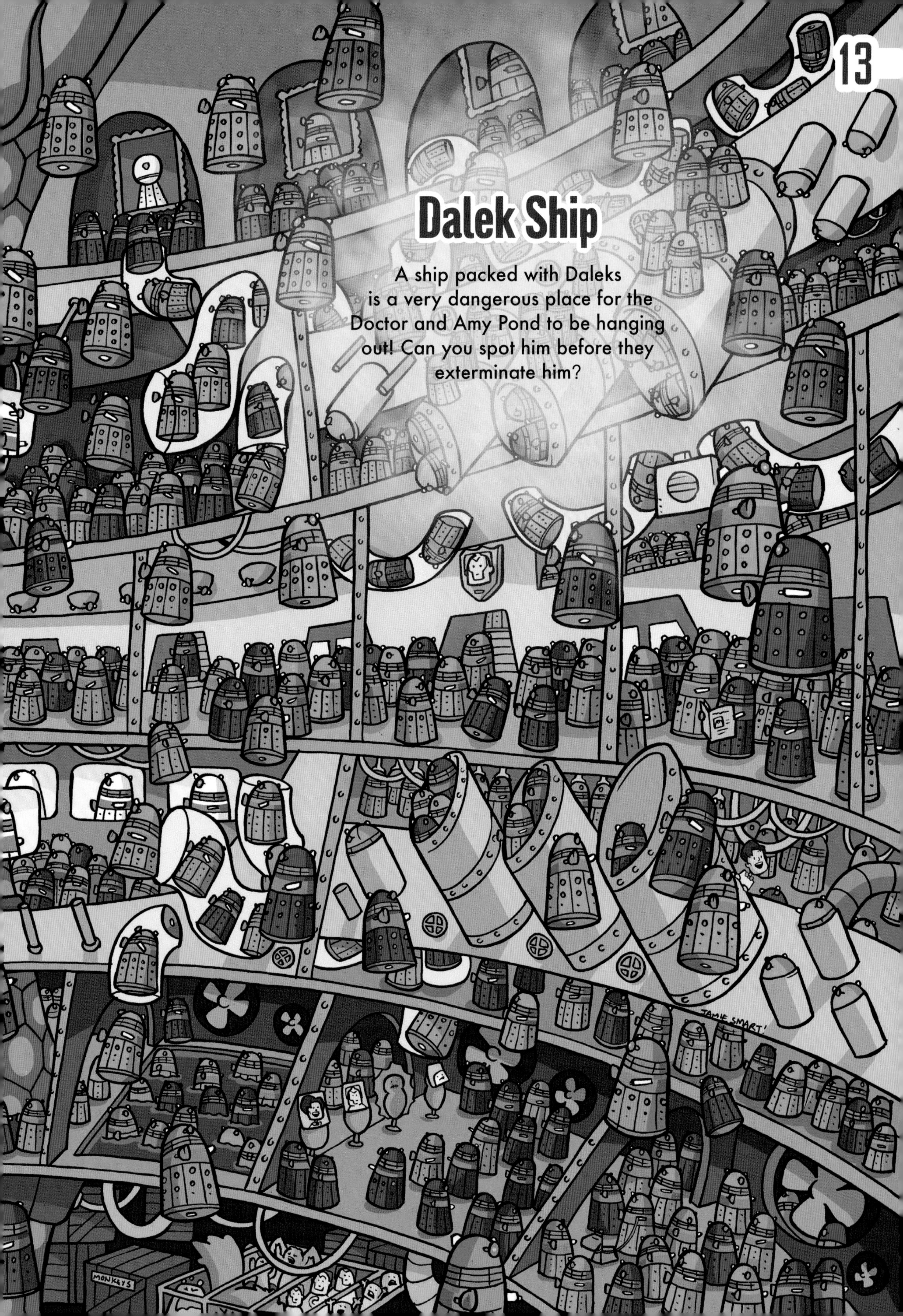
JAMIE SMART!
MONKEYS

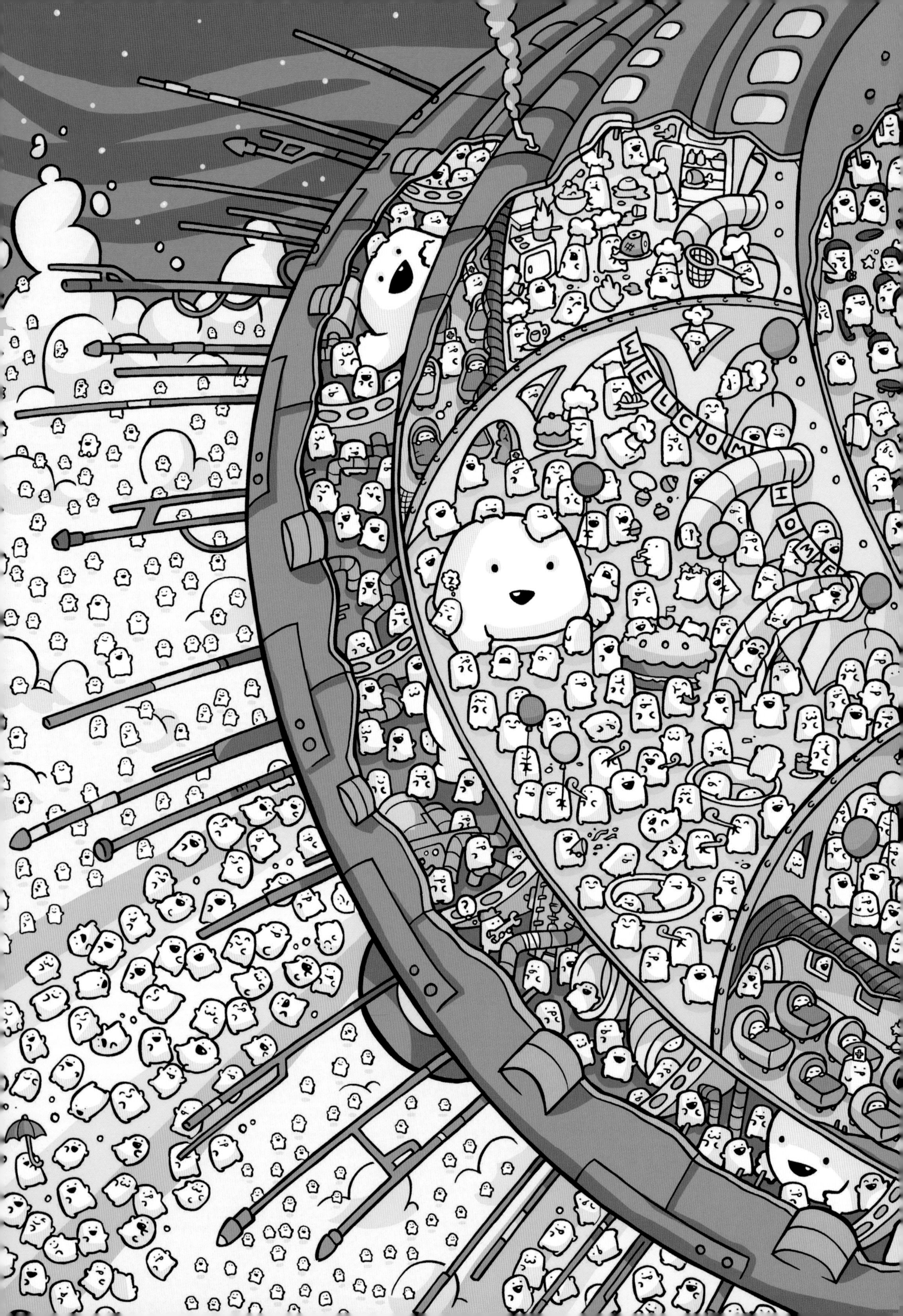
WELCOME
HOME

Adipose Nursery Ship

These cute little critters are having a party. Can you see their uninvited guests?

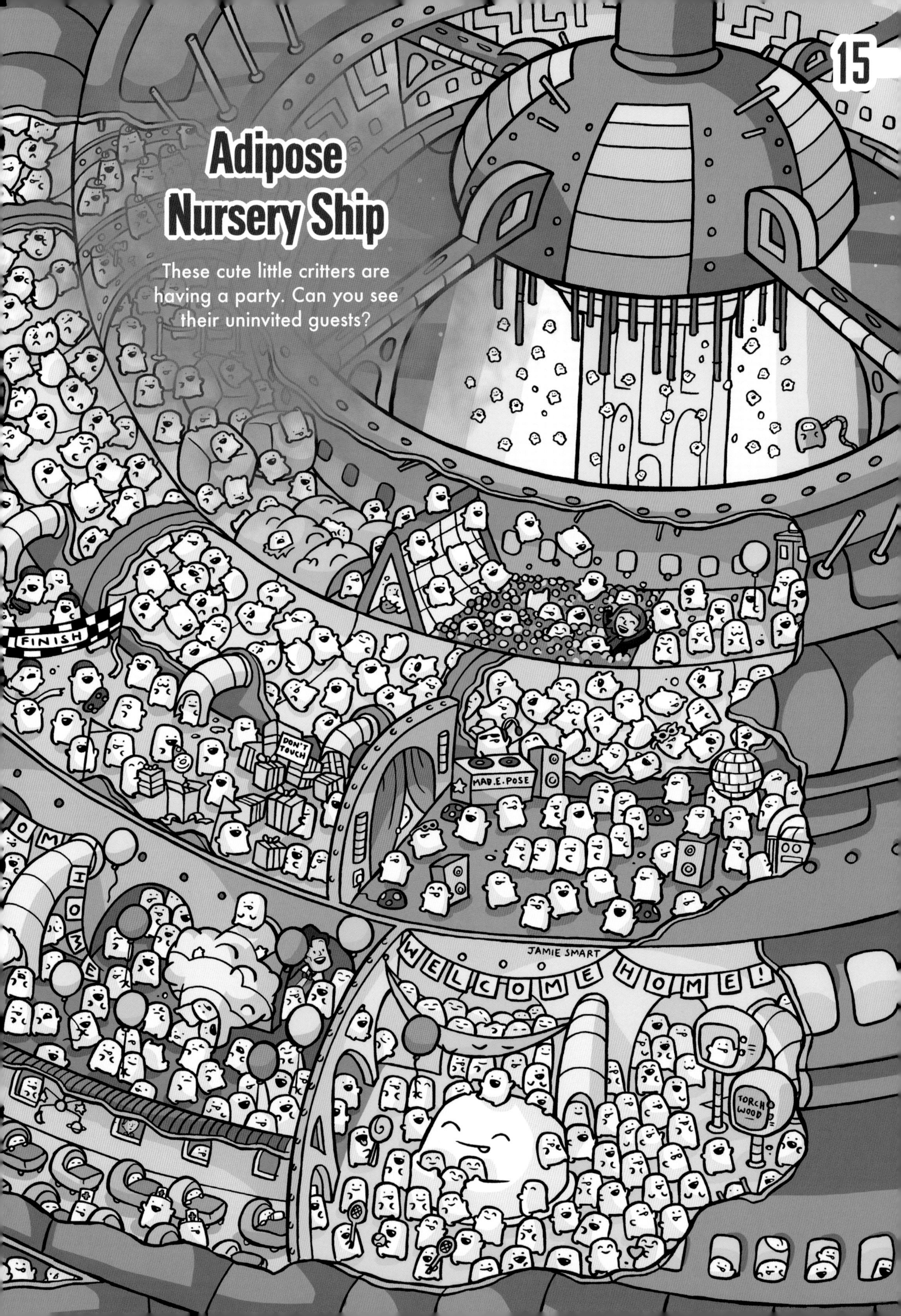
FINISH
DON'T TOUCH
MAD.E.POSE
HOME
WELCOME HOME!
JAMIE SMART
TORCH WOOD

Cyberfactory

Find the Time Lord and his friends before the Cybermen delete them!

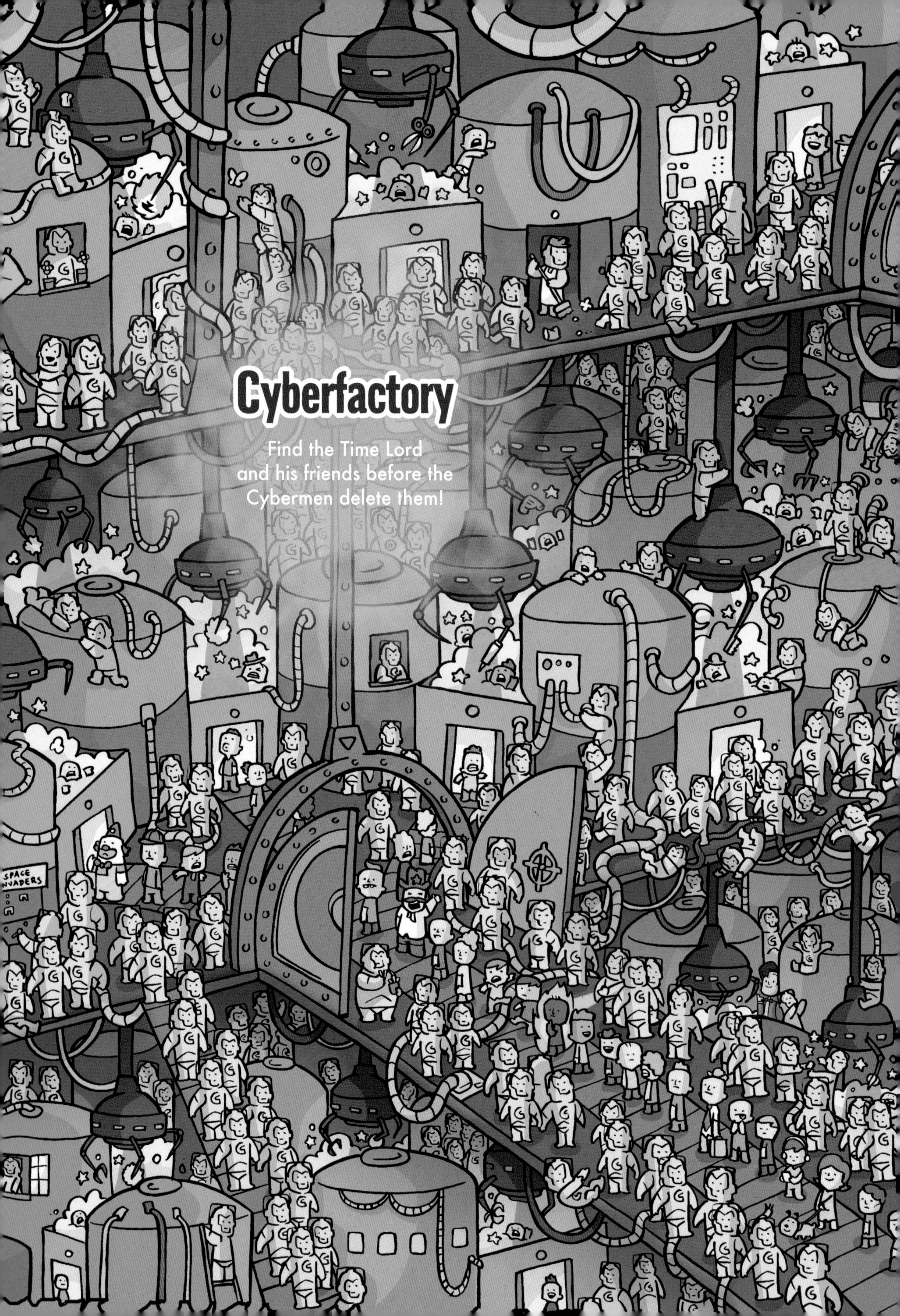
SPACE INVADERS

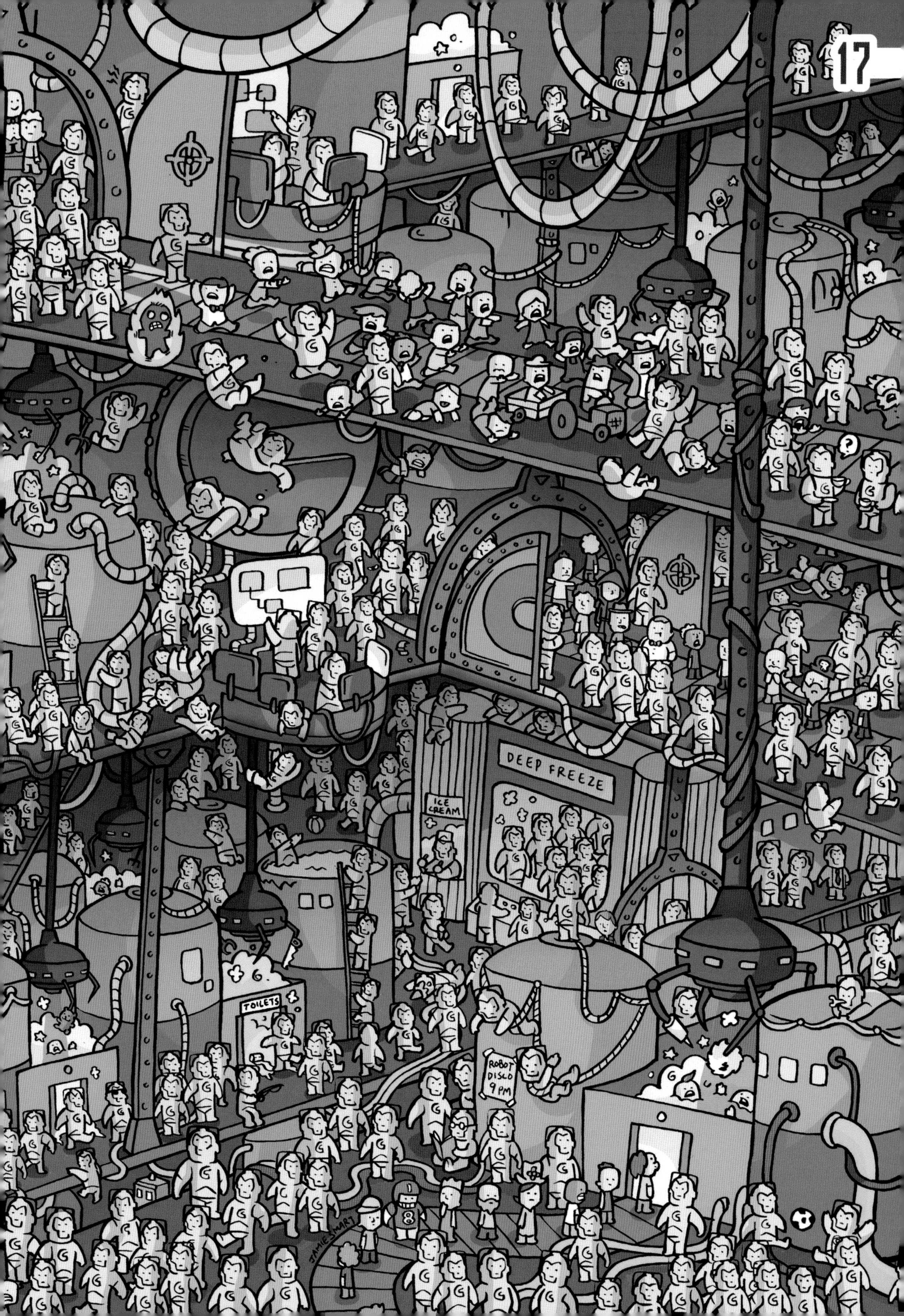
DEEP FREEZE
ICE CREAM
TOILETS
ROBOT DISCO 9PM
JAMIE SMART

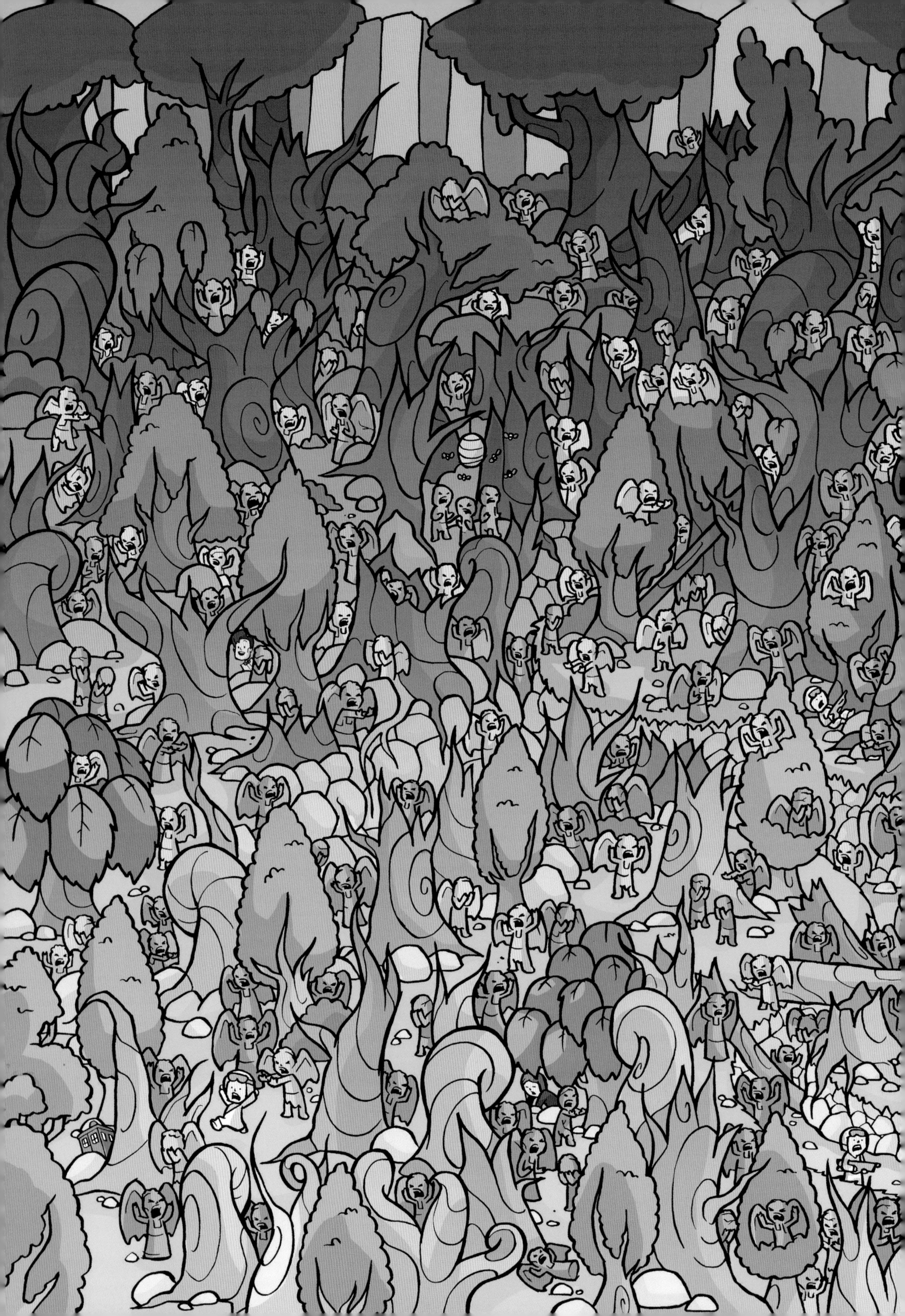

Byzantium Forest

Whatever you do, don't blink until you've found the Doctor and his friends among the trees.

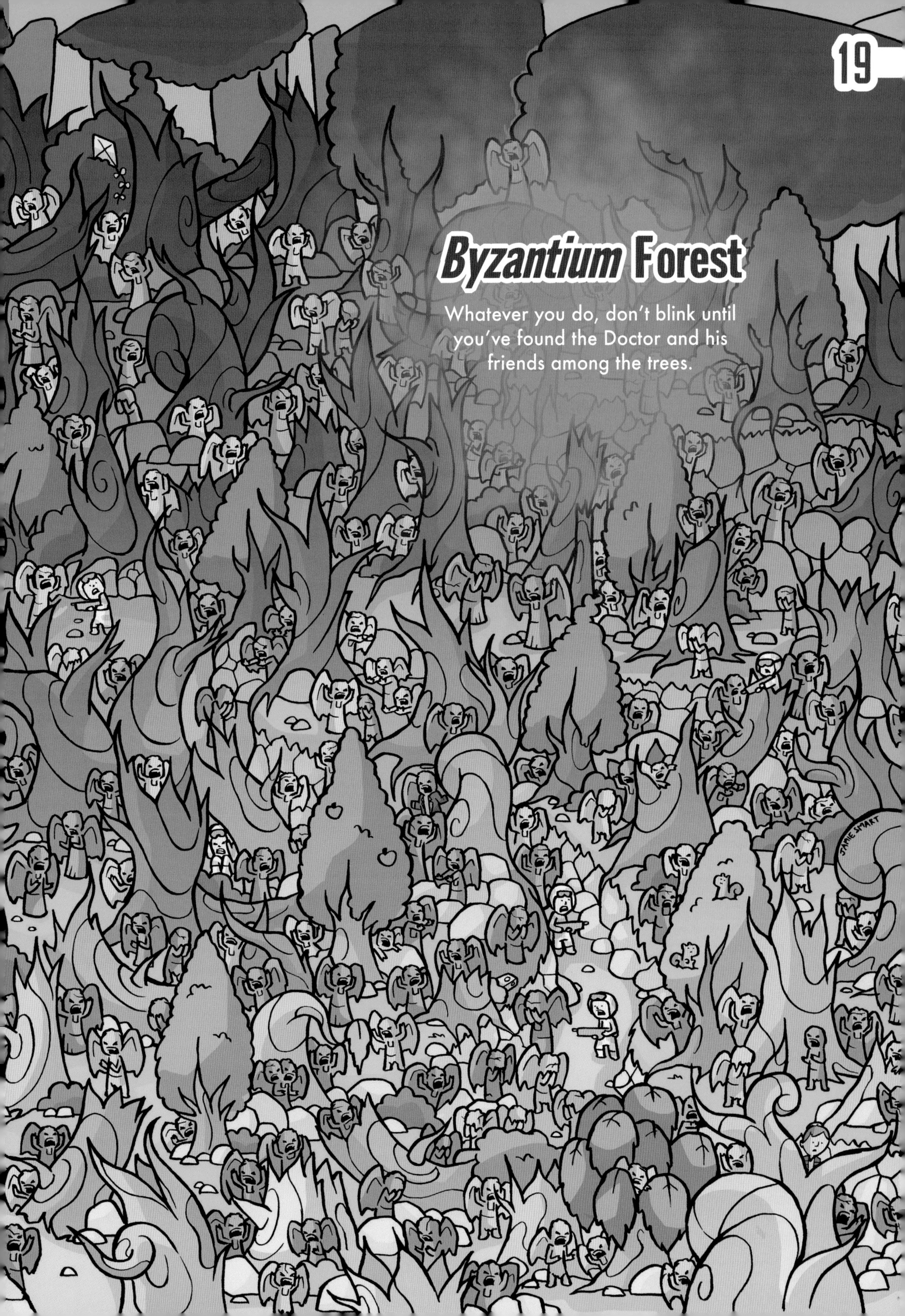
JAMIE SMART

The Ood-Sphere

The Ood are generally pretty friendly, until they turn red-eyed! Can you find the Doctor and his friends before the Ood are possessed?

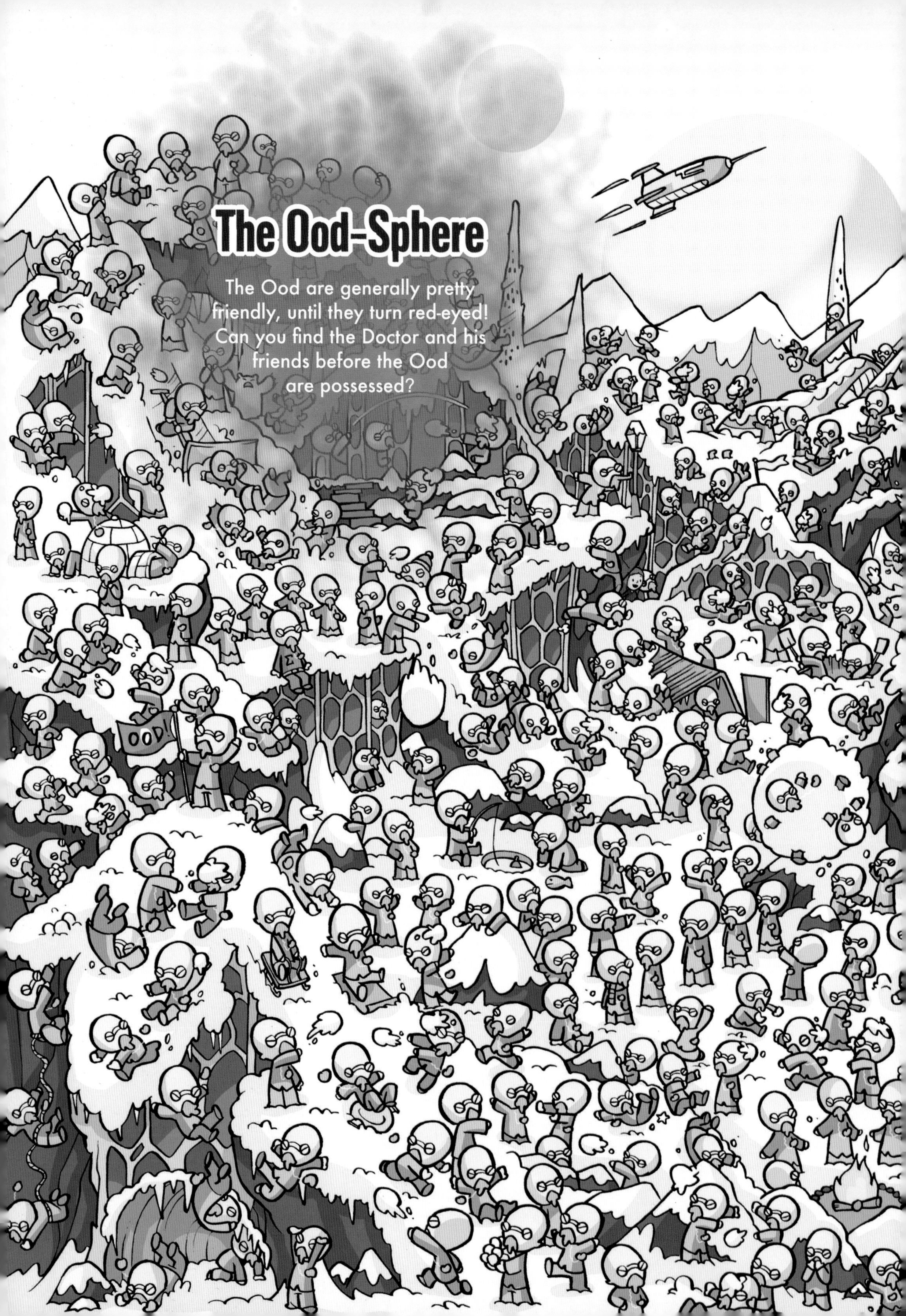
OOD!

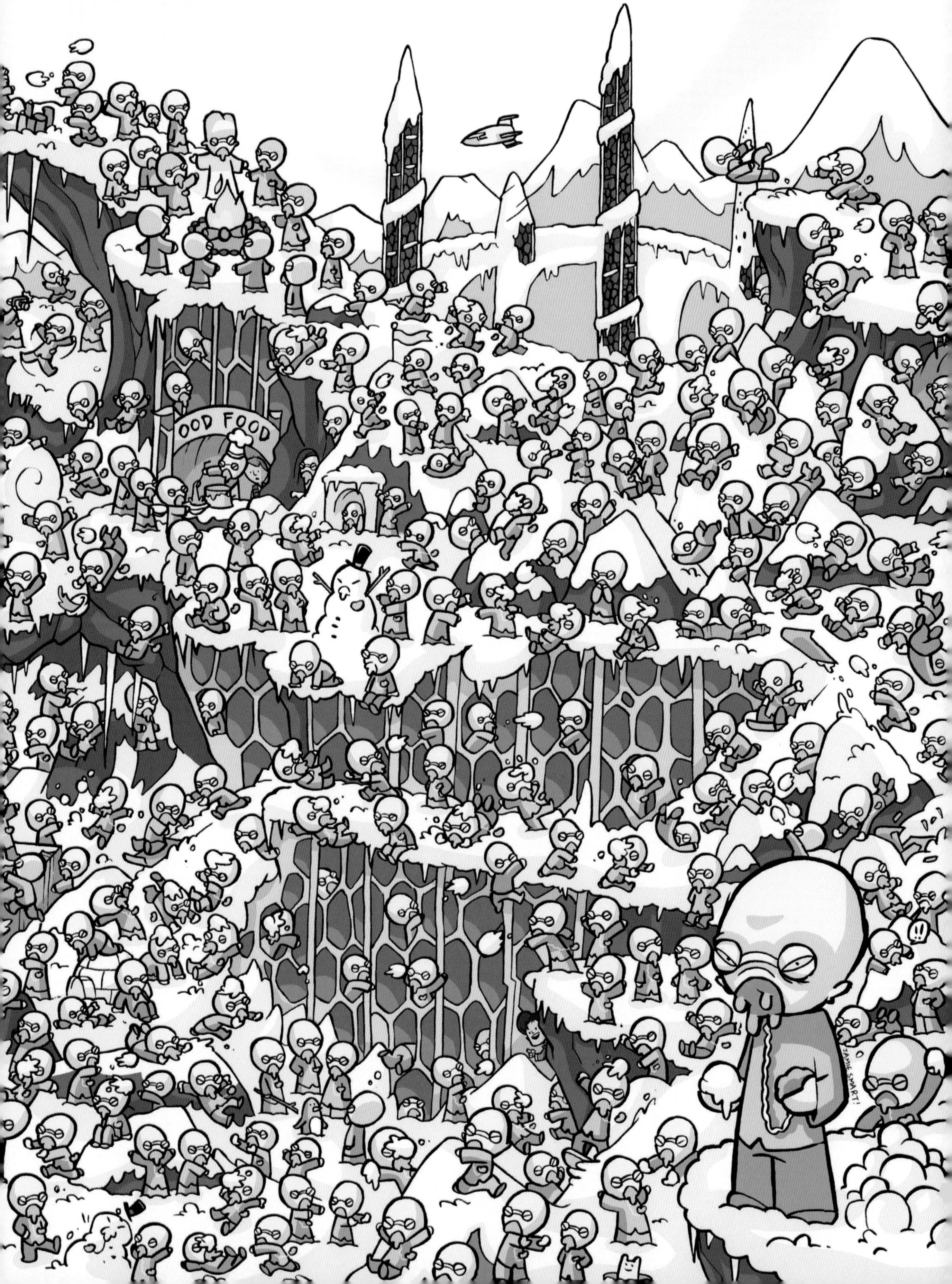
OOD FOOD
JAMIE SMART!

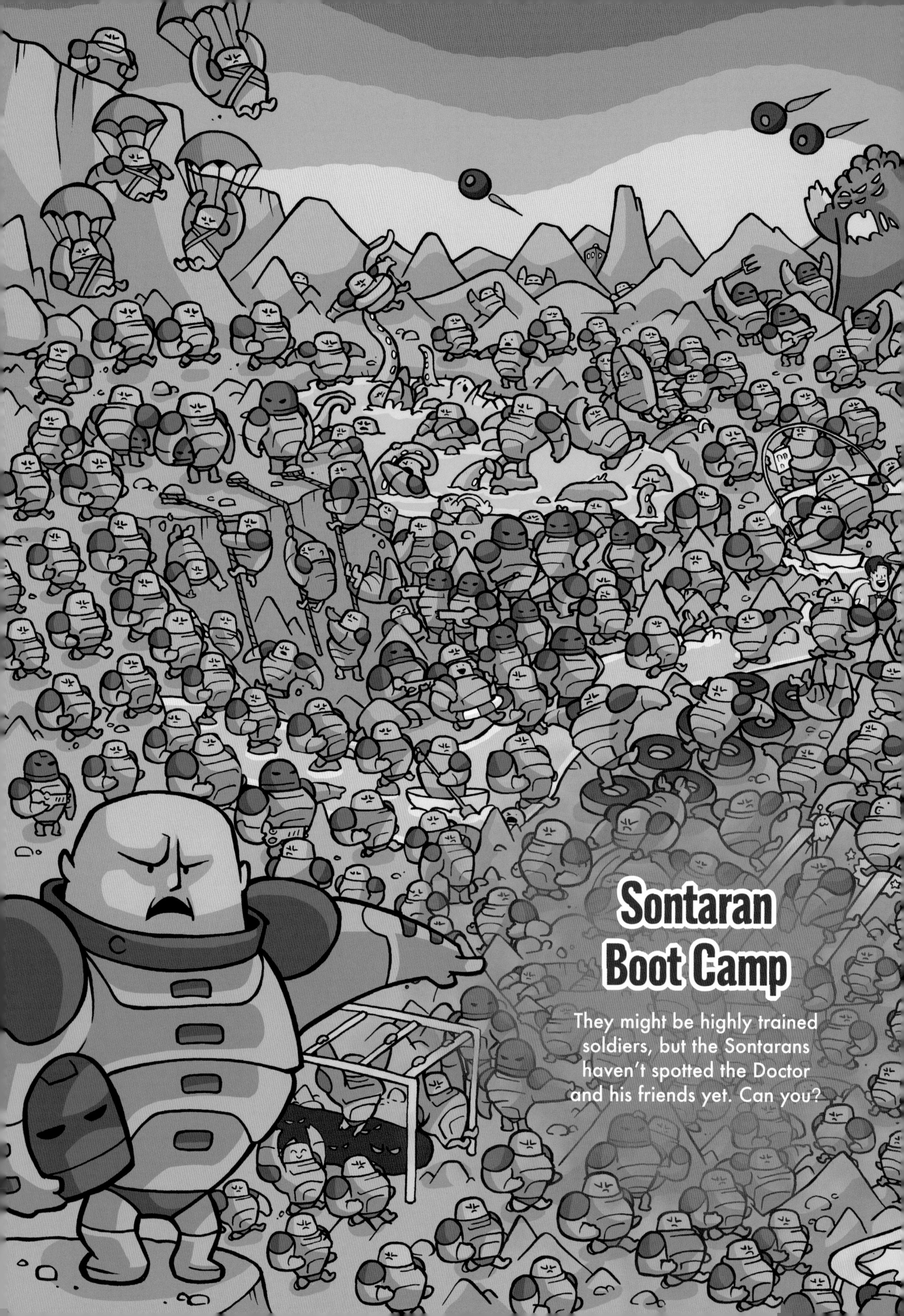

Sontaran Boot Camp

They might be highly trained soldiers, but the Sontarans haven't spotted the Doctor and his friends yet. Can you?

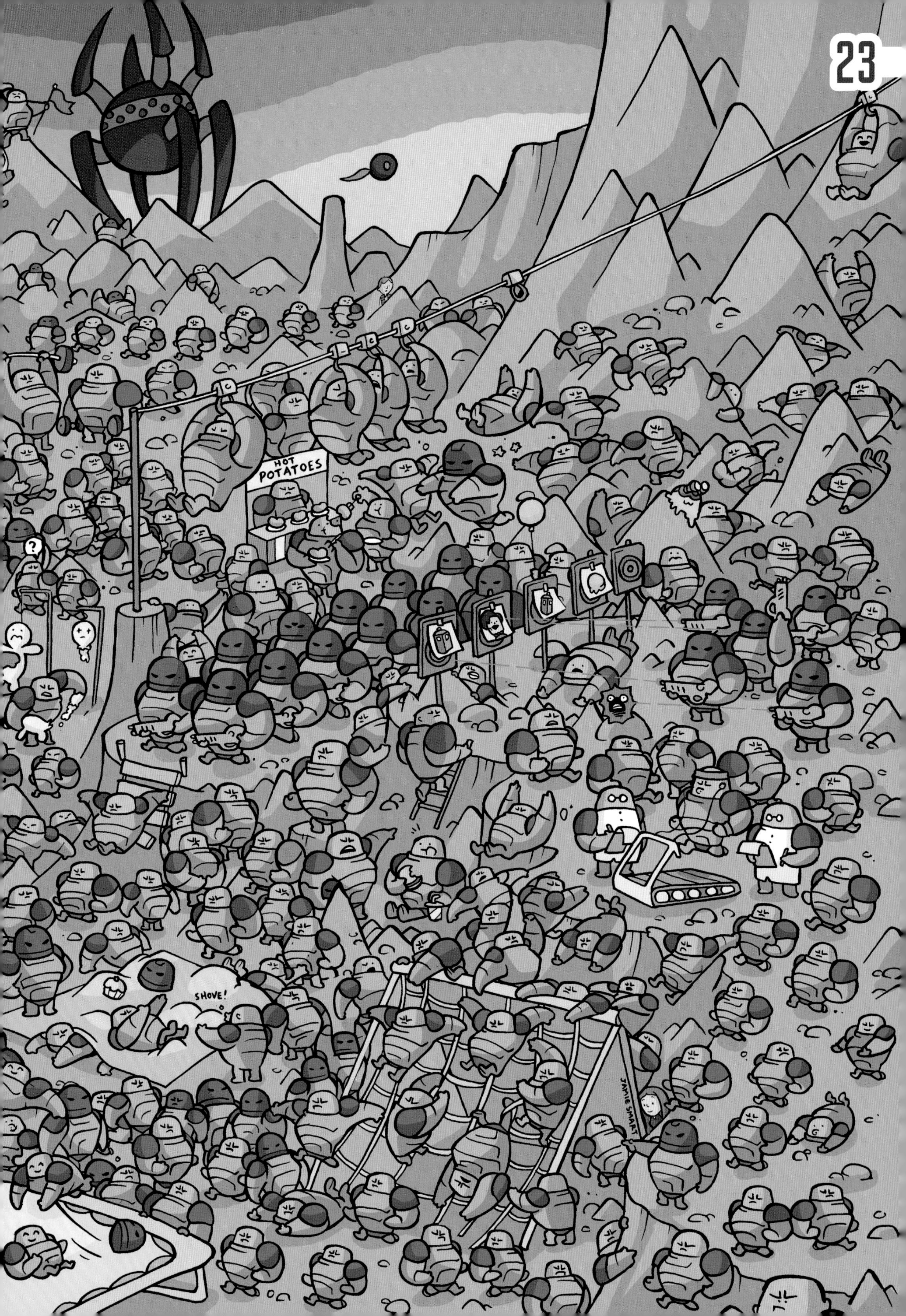
HOT POTATOES
SHOVE!
JAMIE SMART

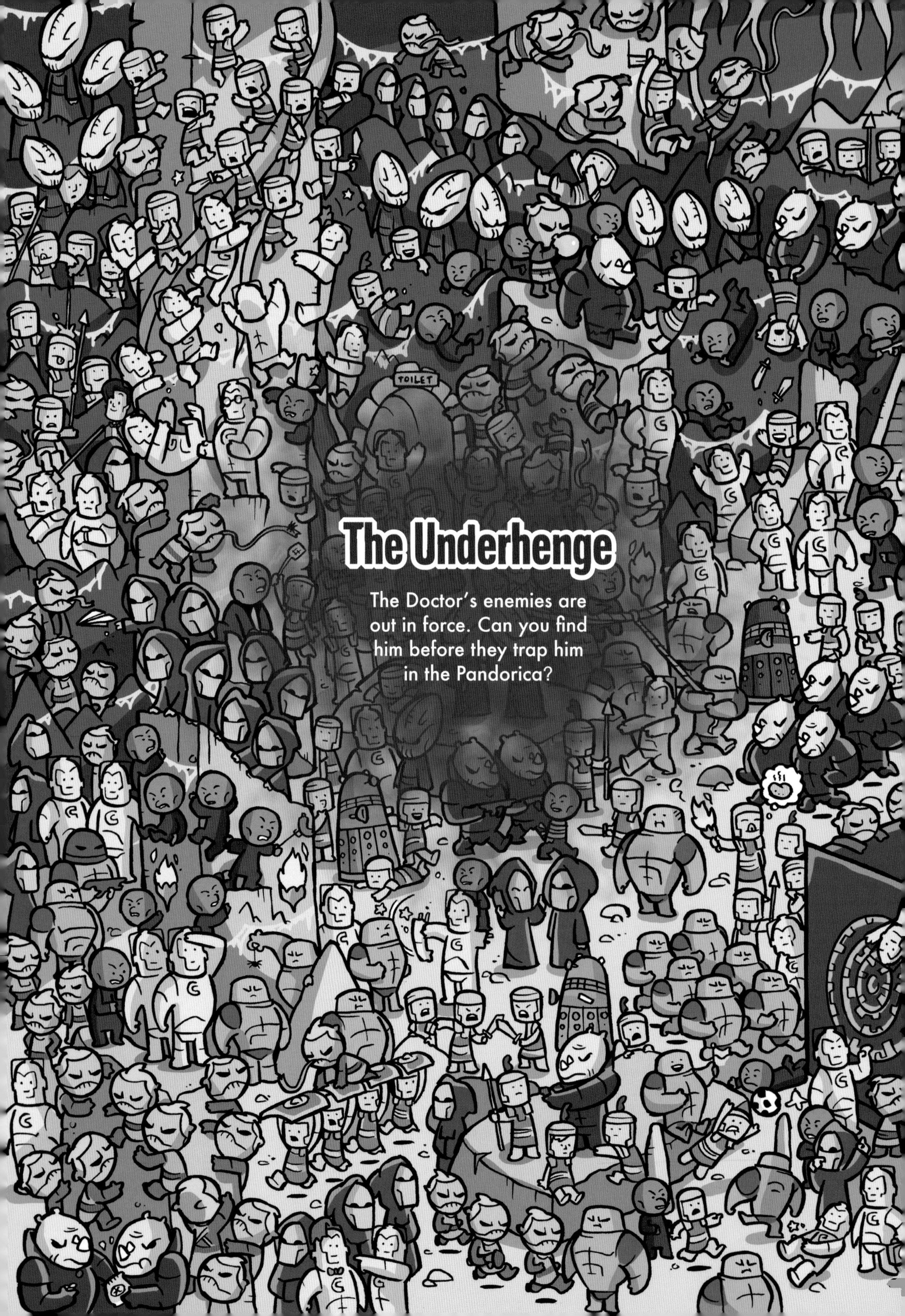
TOILET

The Underhenge

The Doctor's enemies are out in force. Can you find him before they trap him in the Pandorica?

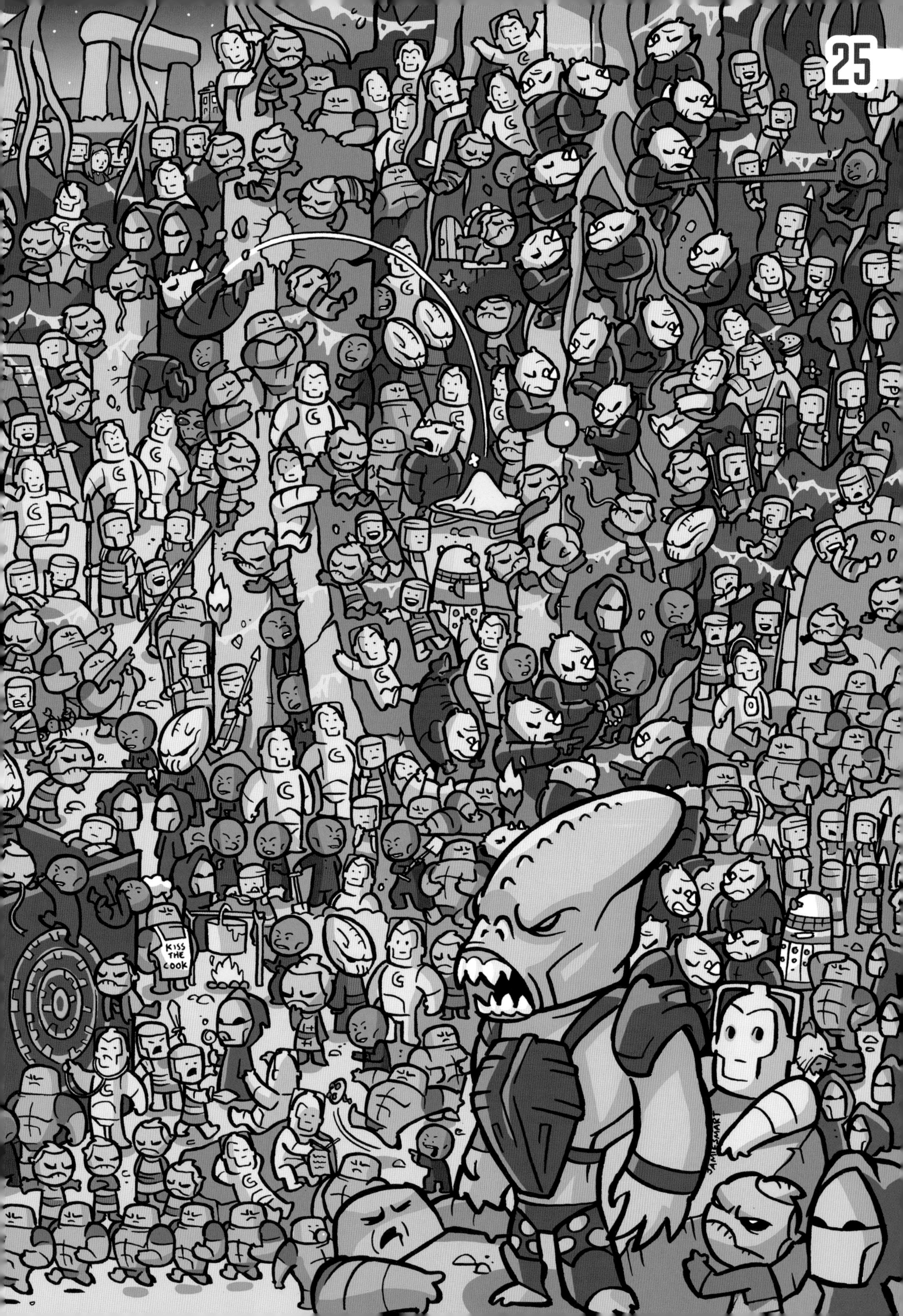
KISS THE COOK
JAMIESMART

Saturnyne

Seek out the Doctor, Amy and Rory in this undersea city of the Saturnynes.

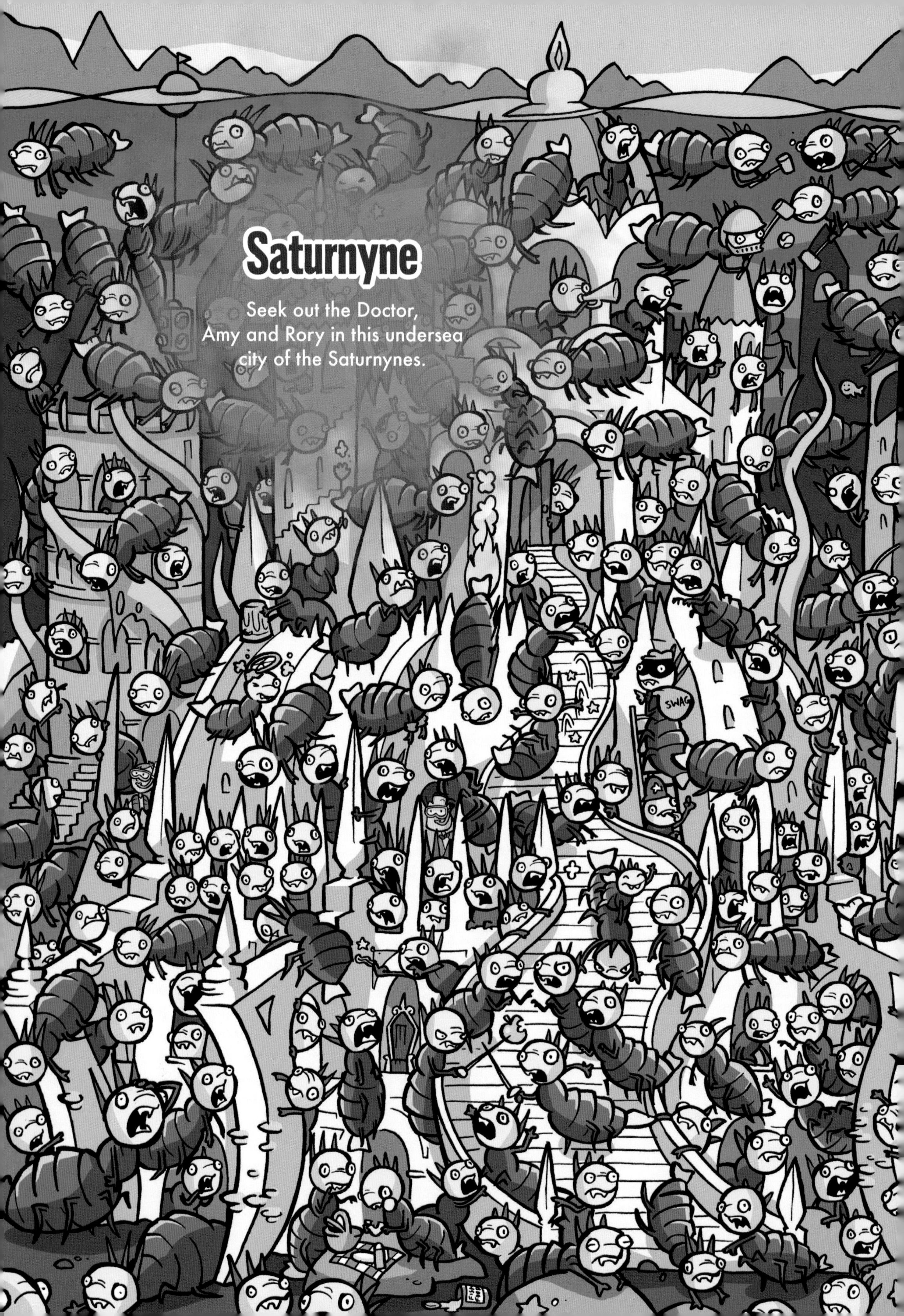
SWAG

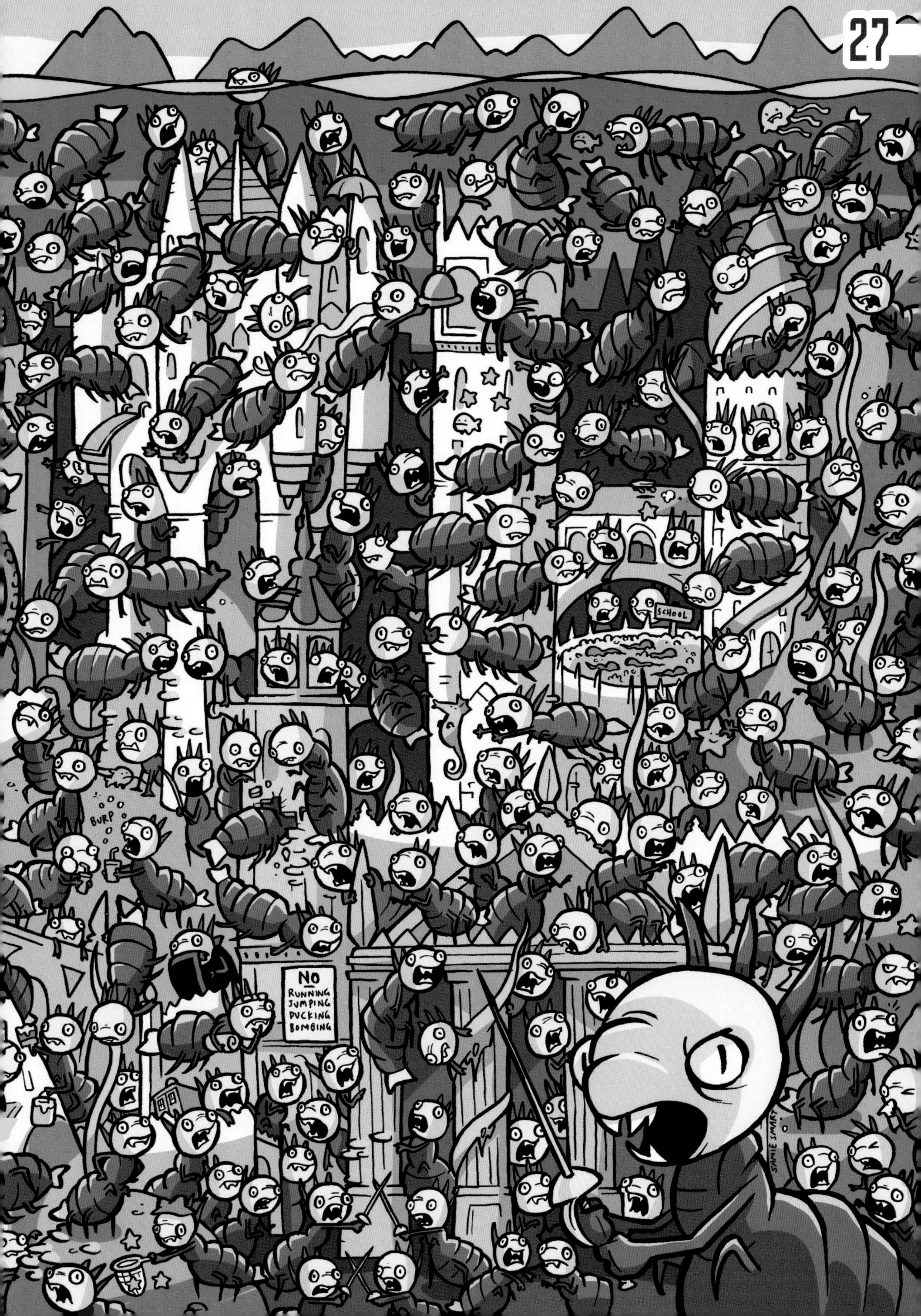
SCHOOL
BURP
NO
RUNNING
JUMPING
DUCKING
BOMBING
SAMIE SMART

The Silence

Watch out for the Silence as you search for the Doctor, Amy and Rory.

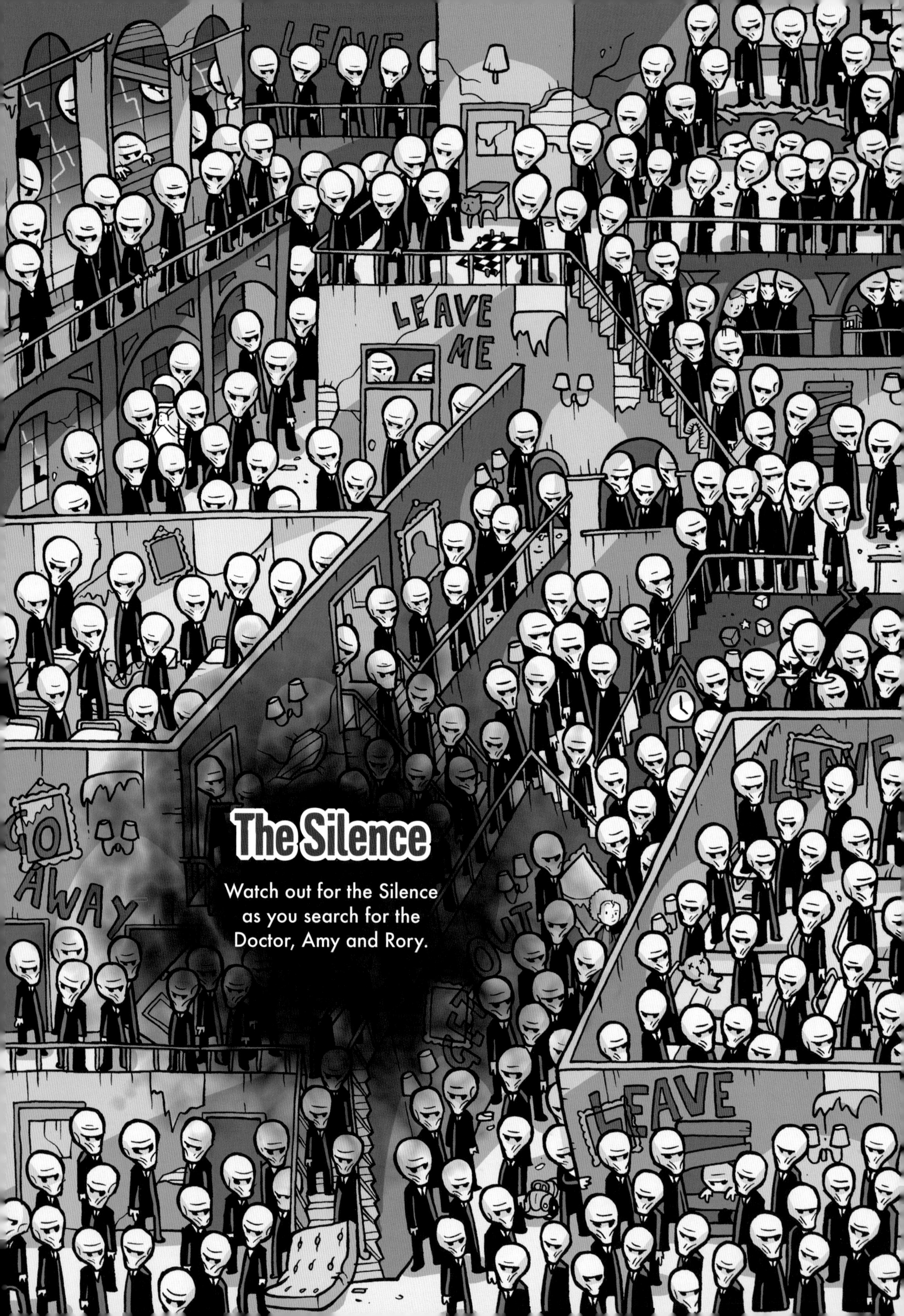
LEAVE ME
AWAY
LEAVE

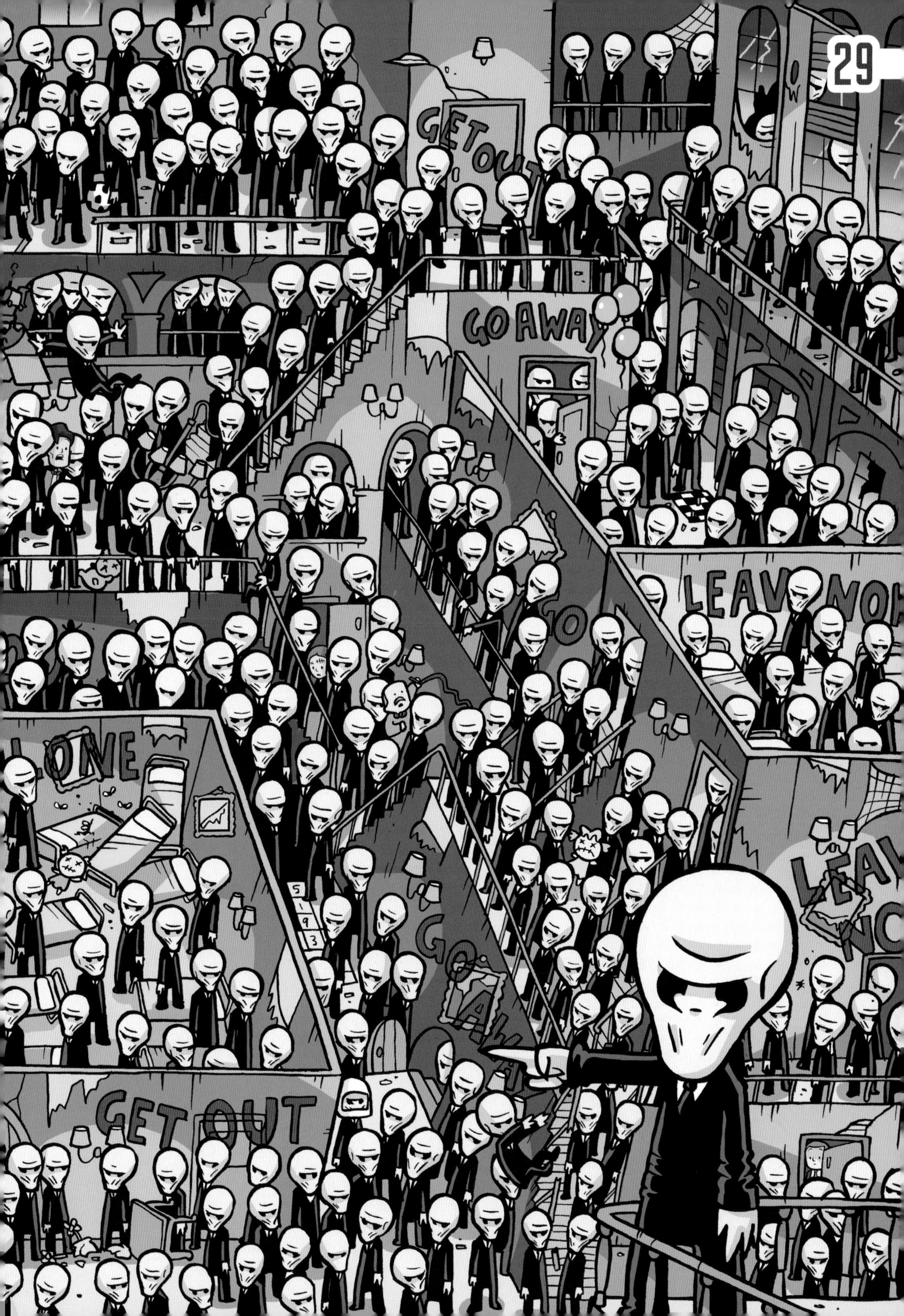
GET OUT
GO AWAY
LEAVE NOW
ALONE
GO
GET OUT

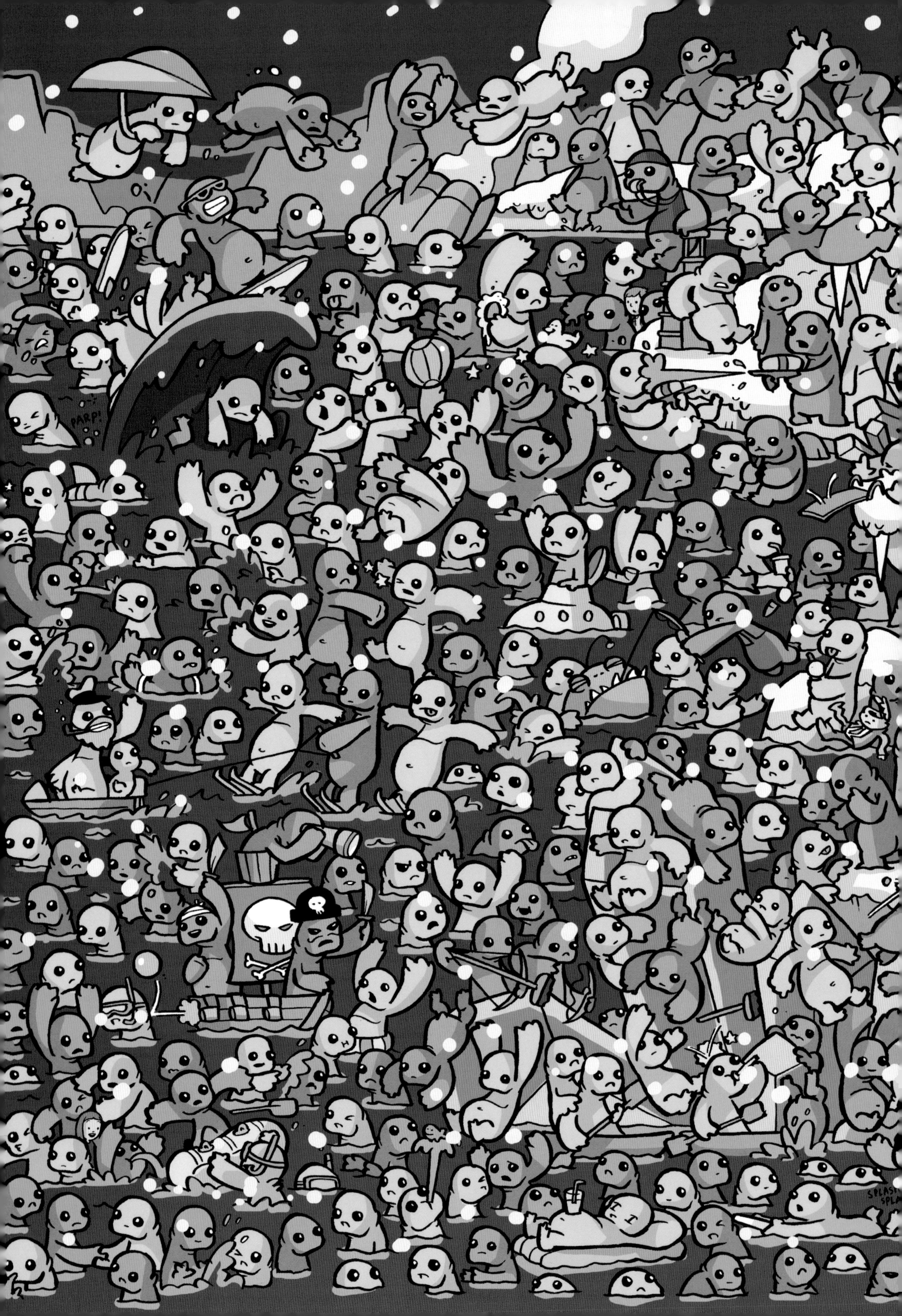
PARP!

The Slitheen

Can you find the Doctor, Amy and Rory in the time it takes the Slitheen to spell Raxacoricofallapatorius?

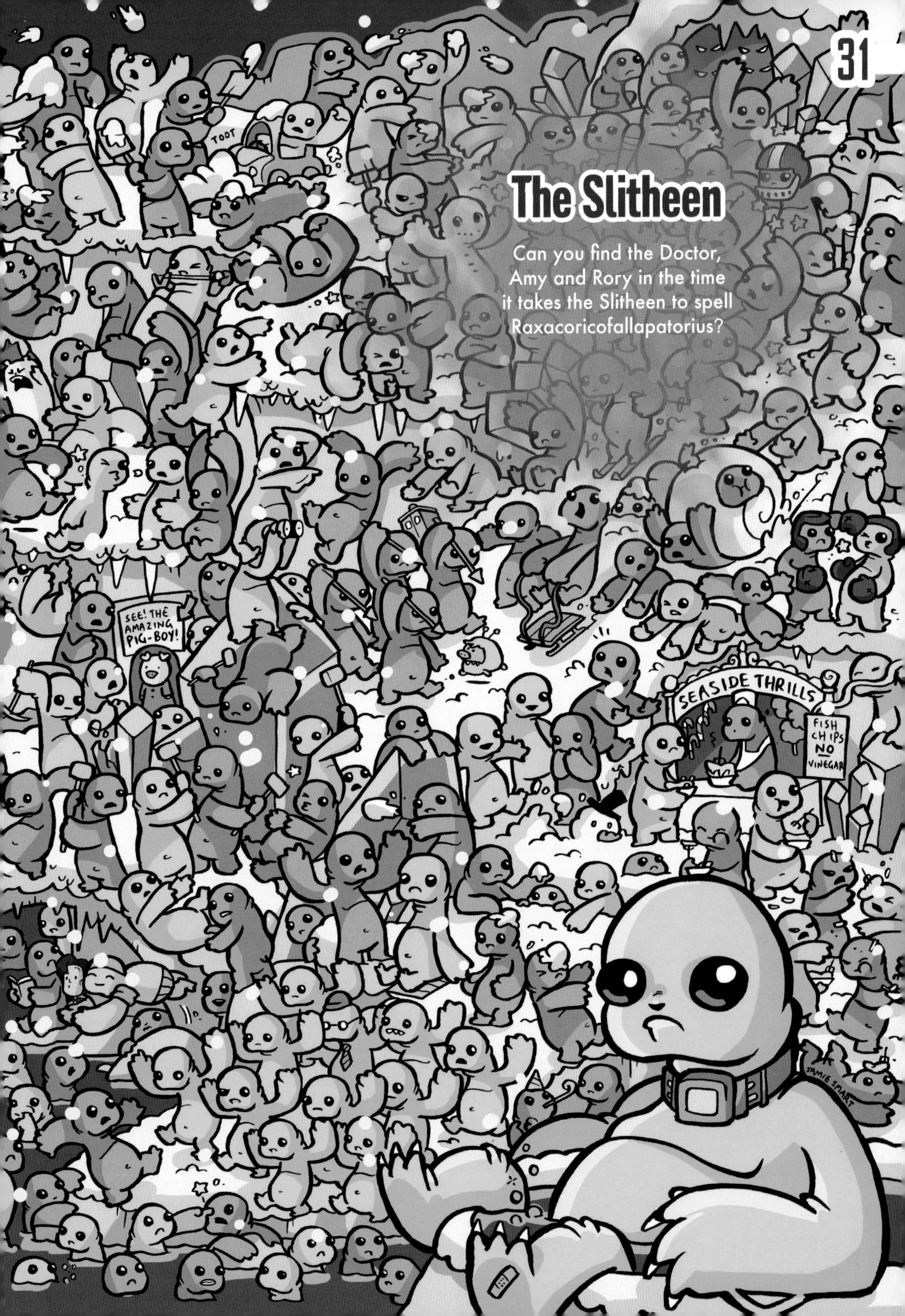
TOOT
SEE! THE AMAZING PIG-BOY!
SEASIDE THRILLS
FISH CHIPS NO VINEGAR
JAMIE SMART

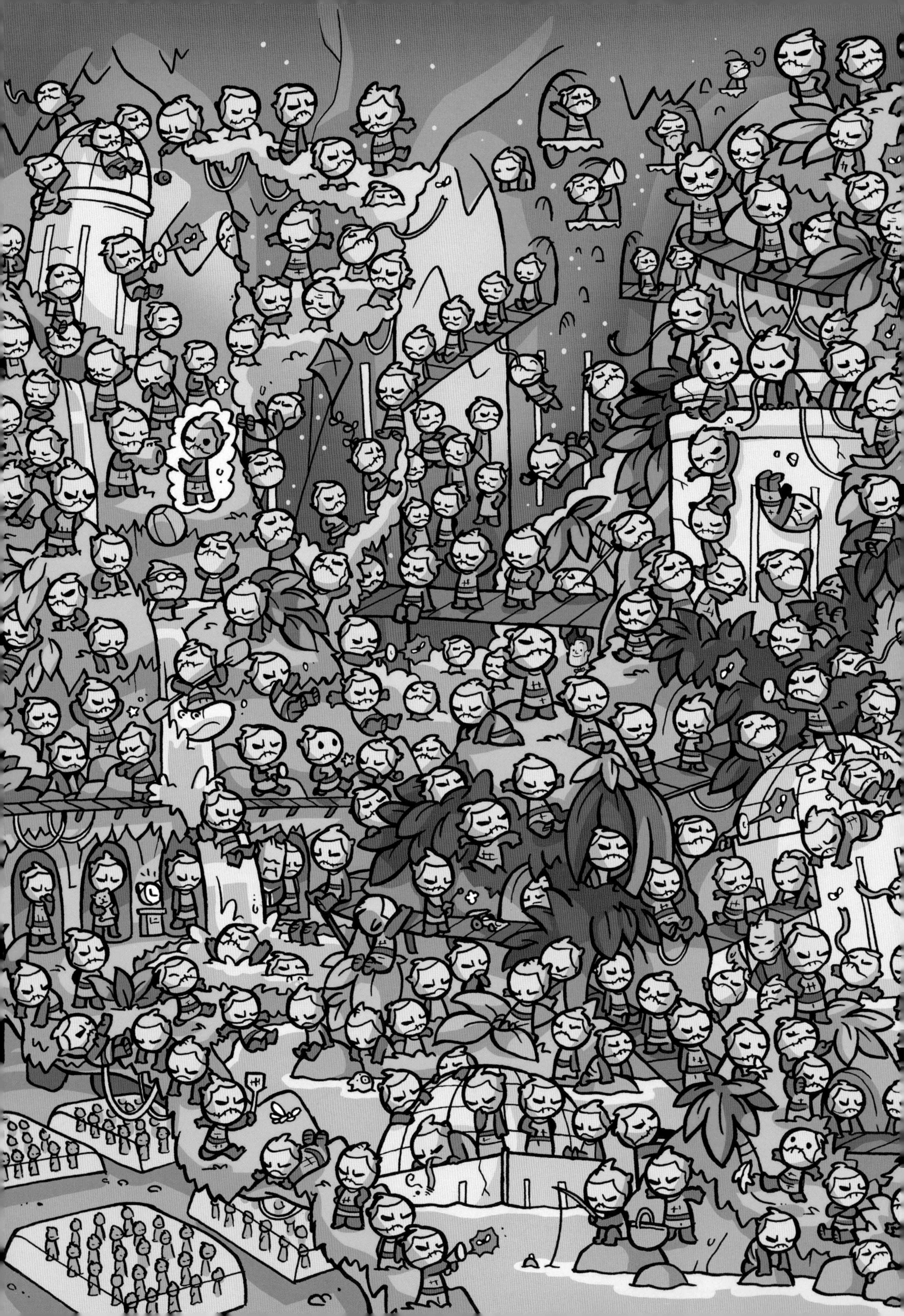

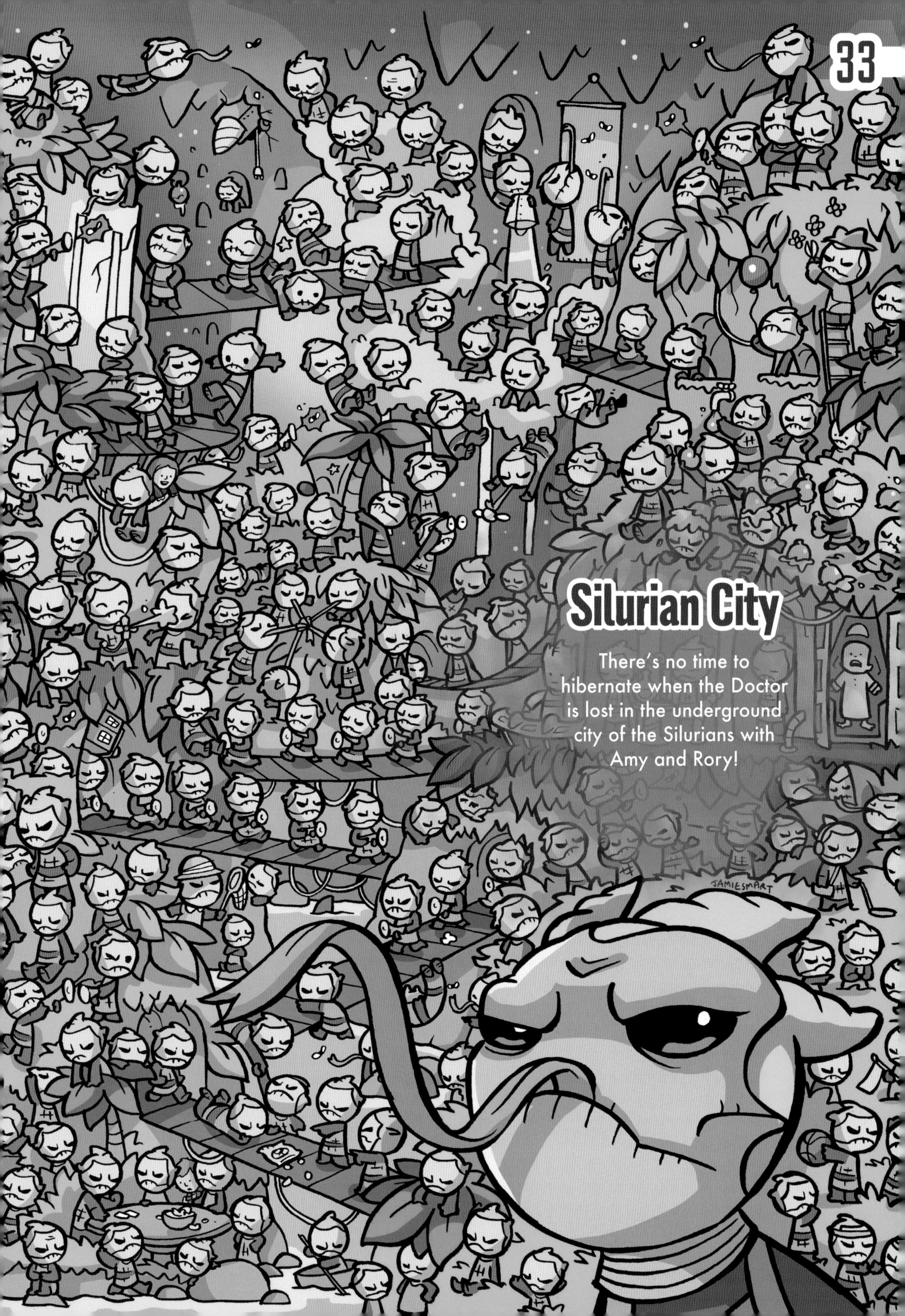
JAMIESMART

Silurian City

There's no time to hibernate when the Doctor is lost in the underground city of the Silurians with Amy and Rory!

More to Find...

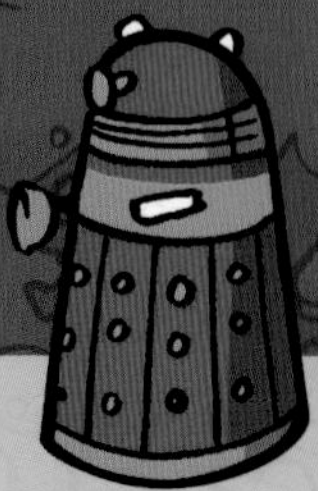

Judoon on the Moon

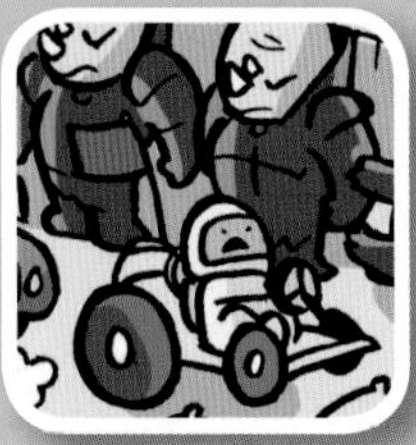

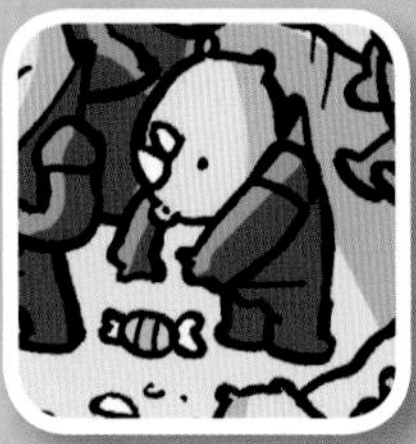

- Sunbathing Judoon
- Four US astronauts
- Drilling Judoon
- Judoon riding on a rocket
- Judoon on a bike
- Two Judoon playing chess
- Judoon holding an oar
- Green sweet
- Two Judoon boxing
- 'Wanted dead or alive' poster

Dalek Ship

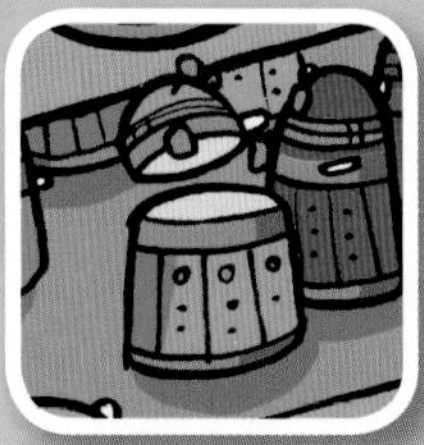

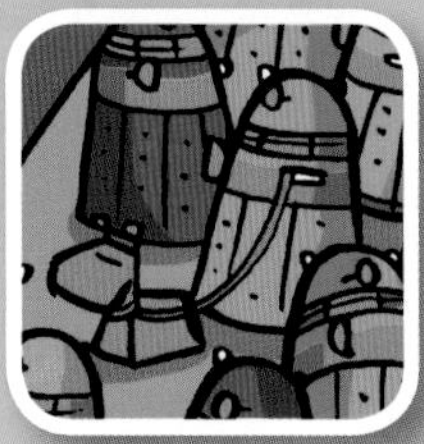

- Cyberman head on a wall plaque
- Box of monkeys
- Dalek reading a newspaper
- Doctor target practice
- Two Weeping Angels
- Portrait of Davros
- Dalek Supreme (not on a screen)
- K-9
- Open Dalek Strategist casing
- Jammie Dodger

Adipose Nursery Ship

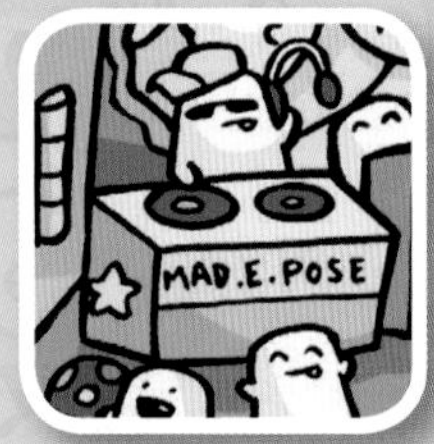
MAD.E.POSE

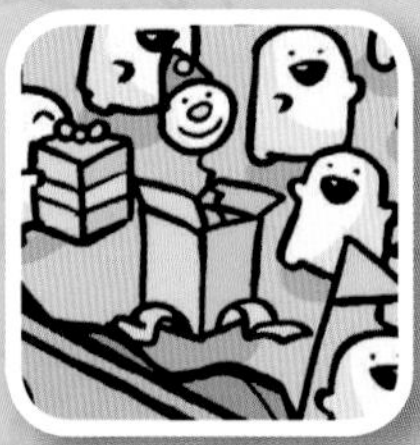

- Adipose in a spacesuit
- Adipose with an umbrella
- Clown balloon
- Adipose with a giant lollipop
- Adipose in star-shaped glasses
- Eight Adipose nurses
- Adipose DJ
- Pan on fire
- Adipose with a spanner
- Two Adipose playing tennis

Cyberfactory

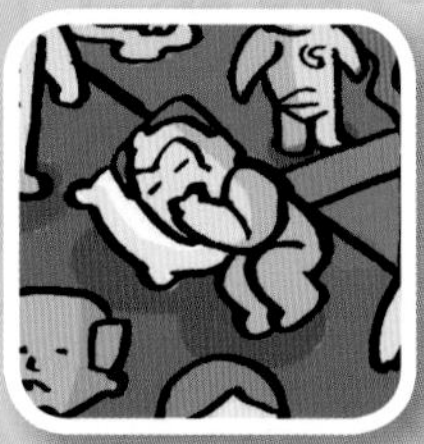

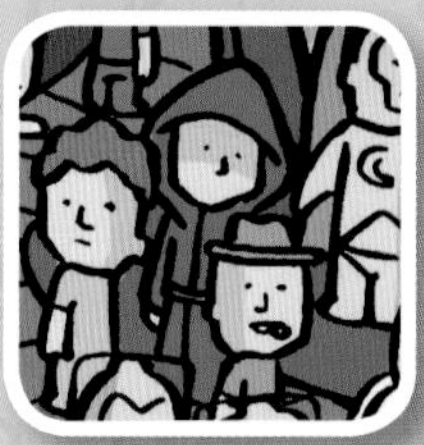

- Pirate
- 'Robot disco 9pm' sign
- Sleeping Cyberman
- Teddy bear
- Cyberman wearing a suit and tie
- Clown
- Two Cybermen playing football
- Cyberman selling ice creams
- Winder
- Cyberman eating toast

Byzantium Forest

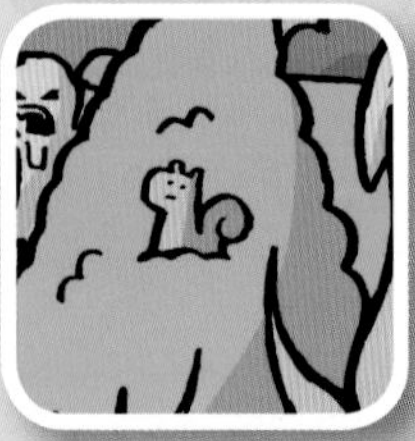

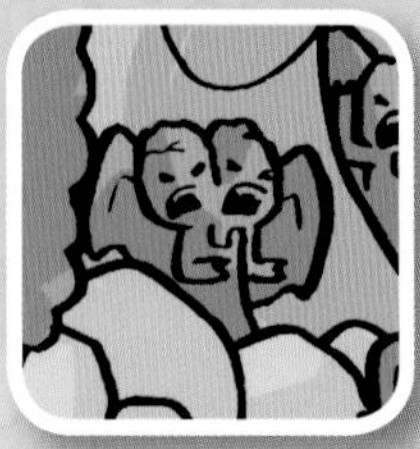

- Two squirrels
- Eight Clerics
- Kite
- Weeping Angel wearing the Doctor's jacket
- A tree with two apples
- Two-headed Angel
- Beehive
- Weeping Angel in a tree stump
- Weeping Angel fallen over
- Jamie Smart's signature

The Ood-Sphere

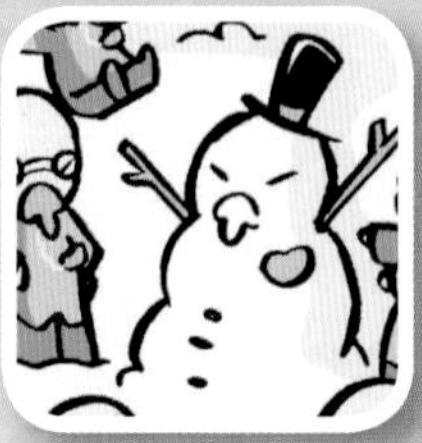

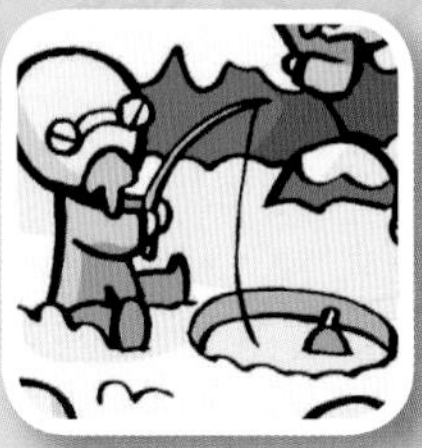

- Ood Sigma
- Two snow-Ood
- Ood with its tongue stuck to a lamp post
- Ood wearing a purple bobble hat
- Igloo
- Ood fishing in a hole
- Surfing Ood
- Red-eyed Ood
- Penguin
- Blue flag

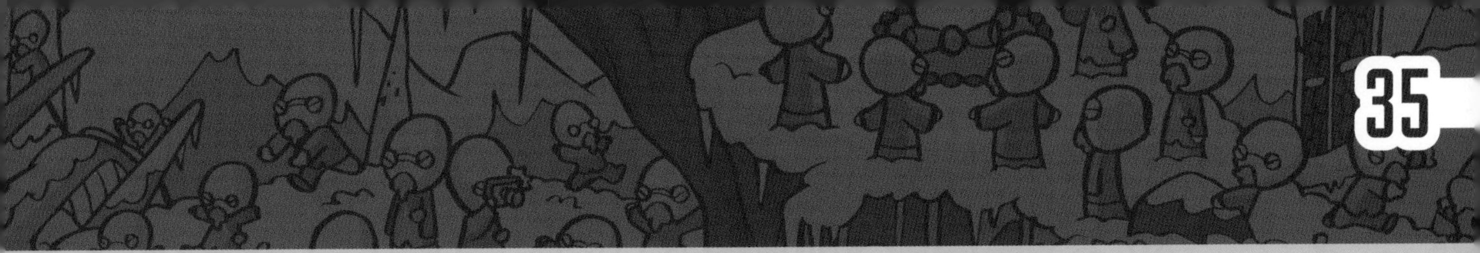

Sontaran Boot Camp

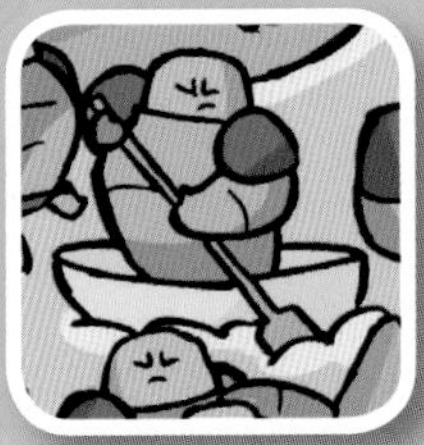

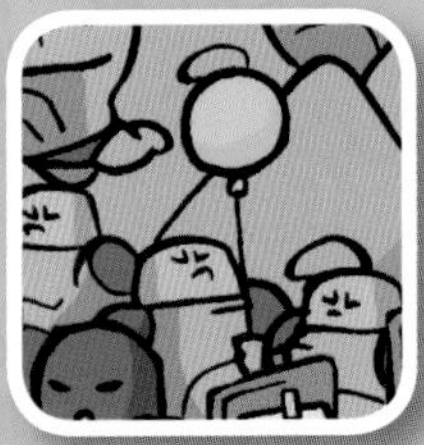

- [ ] Sontaran wearing a rubber ring
- [ ] Hula-hooping Sontaran
- [ ] Cake with a cherry on the top
- [ ] Sontaran holding a red flag
- [ ] Sontaran with a green balloon
- [ ] Rutan spy with binoculars
- [ ] Sontaran lifting weights
- [ ] Three Sontarans in green boats
- [ ] Sontaran diving off a springboard
- [ ] Green clone

Saturnyne

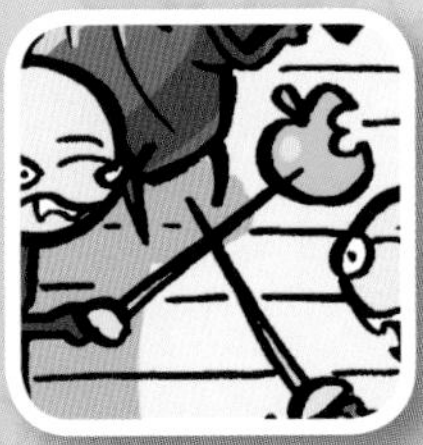

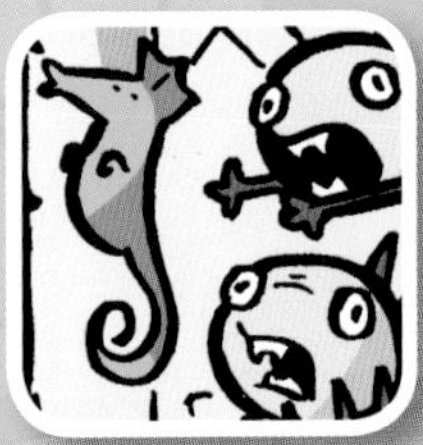

- [ ] Saturnyne carrying a swag bag
- [ ] Apple on a sword
- [ ] Saturnyne catching a star in a net
- [ ] Two smiling starfish
- [ ] Saturnyne with an umbrella
- [ ] Two Saturnyne having a picnic
- [ ] Seahorse
- [ ] Burping Saturnyne
- [ ] Unhappy fish
- [ ] Jar of fish food

The Slitheen

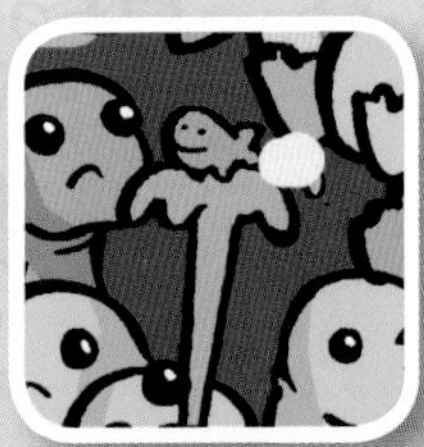

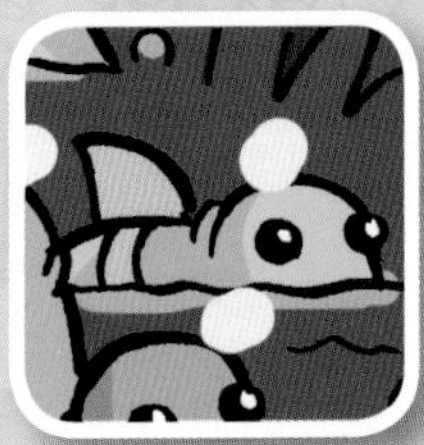

- [ ] Melting snowman
- [ ] Slitheen reading a book
- [ ] Yellow duck
- [ ] Slitheen lifeguard
- [ ] Slitheen with a slingshot
- [ ] Two Slitheen having a water fight
- [ ] Slitheen wearing a shark fin
- [ ] Slitheen blowing a fish into the air
- [ ] Discarded human costume
- [ ] Two Slitheen firing brooms with bows

The Underhenge

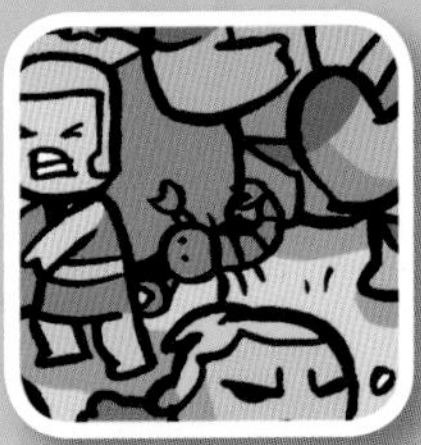

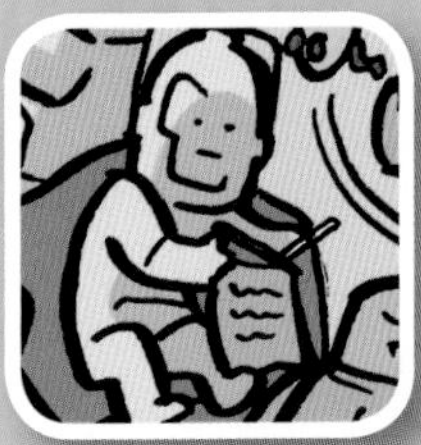

- [ ] Sontaran in a 'Kiss the Cook' apron
- [ ] Judoon on a trampoline
- [ ] Roman thinking about potatoes
- [ ] Cyberman dressed as the Doctor
- [ ] Lobster
- [ ] Roman eating a burger
- [ ] Cyberman knitting
- [ ] Fez
- [ ] Sontaran with a spider
- [ ] Silurian blowing up a balloon

The Silence

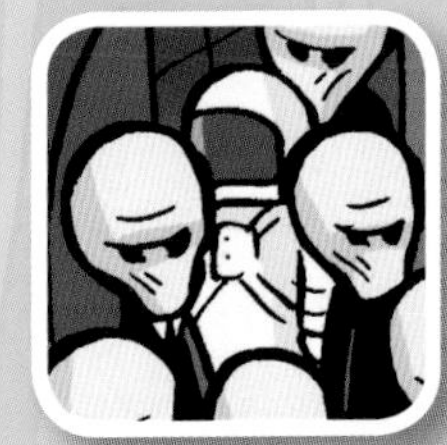

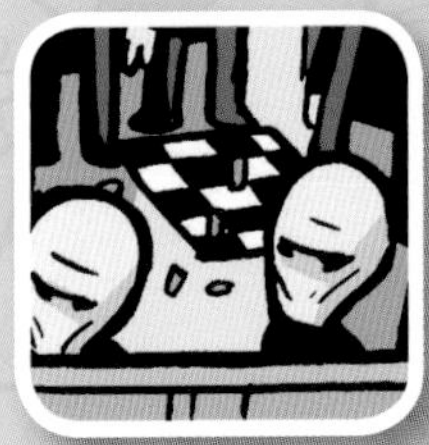

- [ ] Ginger cat
- [ ] Silent in an astronaut helmet
- [ ] Yellow car
- [ ] Astronaut
- [ ] Snake
- [ ] Two chessboards
- [ ] Slinky
- [ ] Silent in a puddle
- [ ] Toybox
- [ ] Man drawing on the wall

Silurian City

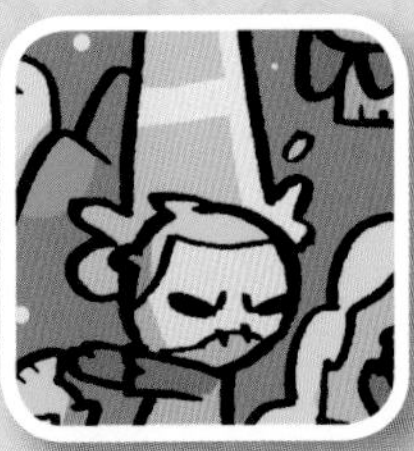

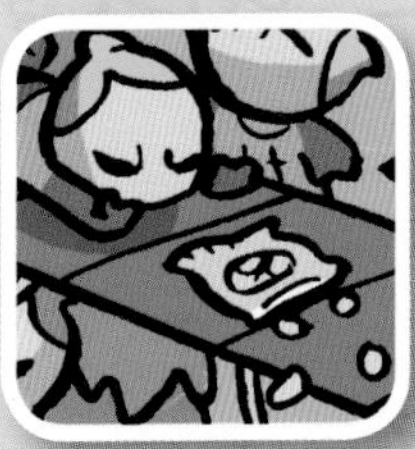

- [ ] Silurian with a teddy bear
- [ ] Three Silurians playing basketball
- [ ] Silurian driving a remote-controlled car
- [ ] Silurian tipping a bucket of water over another Silurian
- [ ] Five tongue-tied Silurians
- [ ] Silurian wearing safari clothes
- [ ] Silurian Elder
- [ ] Silurian with a yo-yo
- [ ] Silurian dropping a packet of crisps
- [ ] Silurian reading a book

Spot the Difference

There are ten differences between these pictures. Can you spot them?

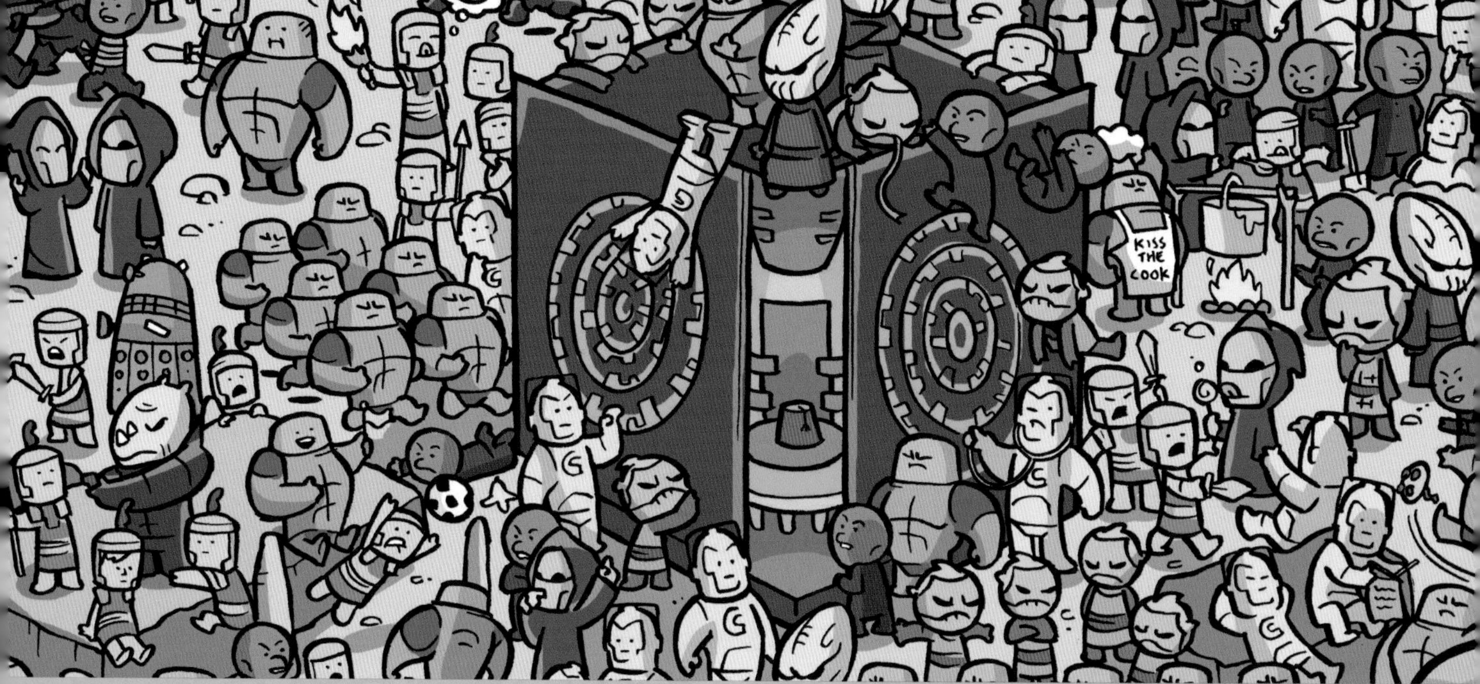
KISS THE COOK

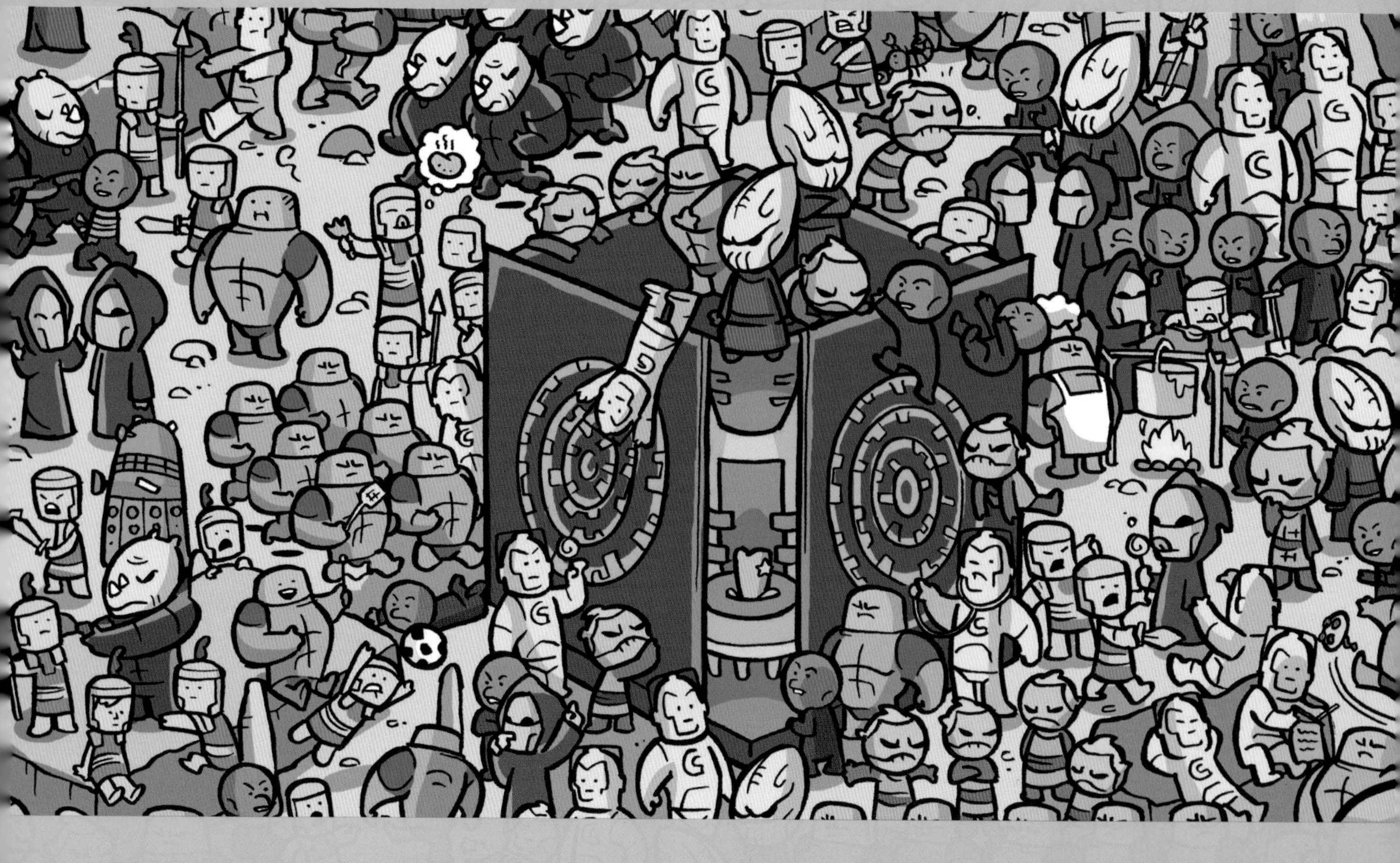

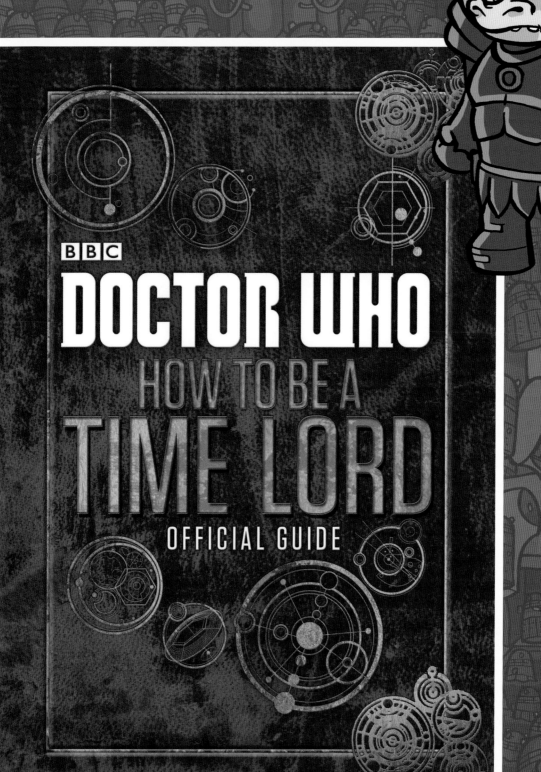

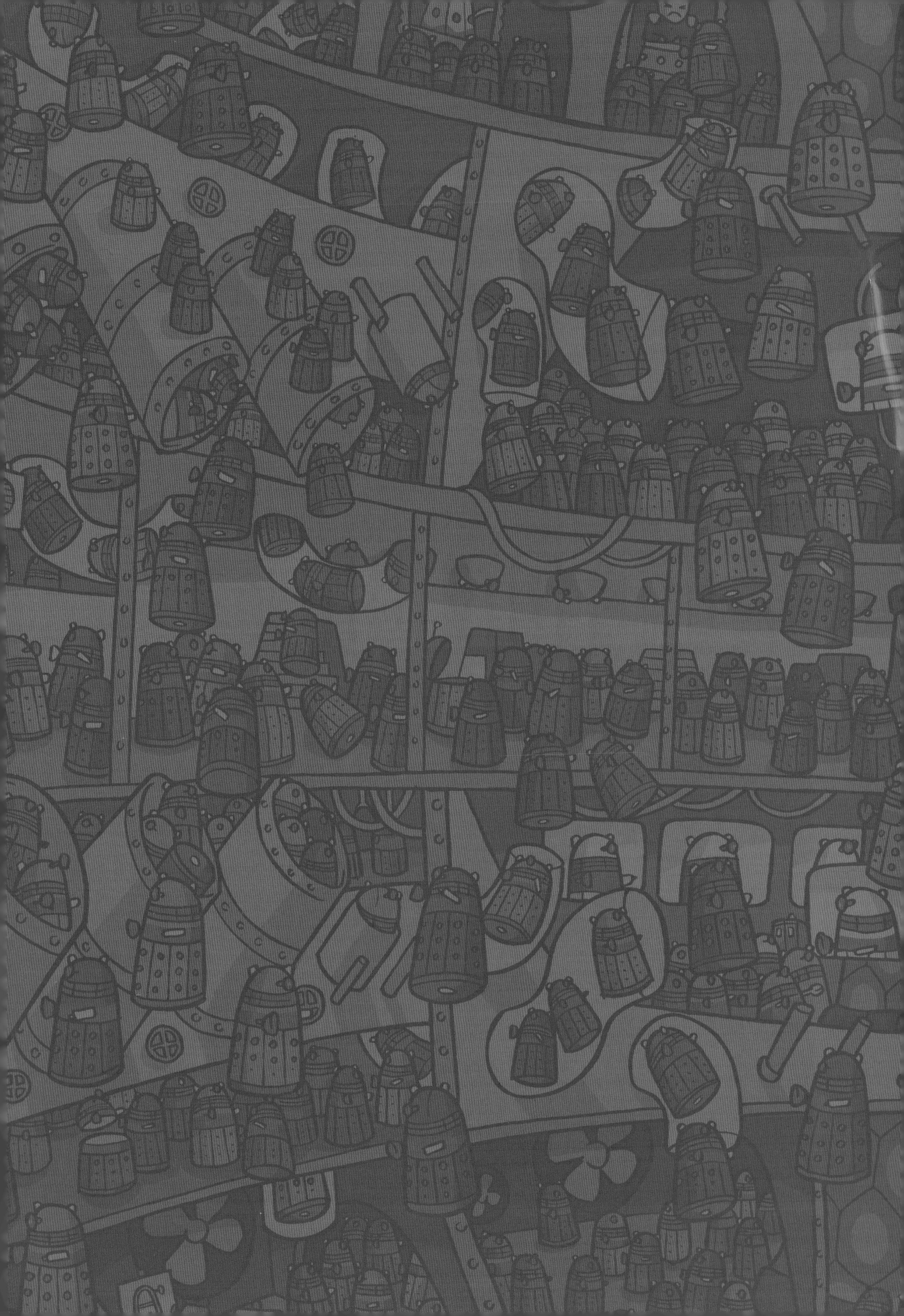

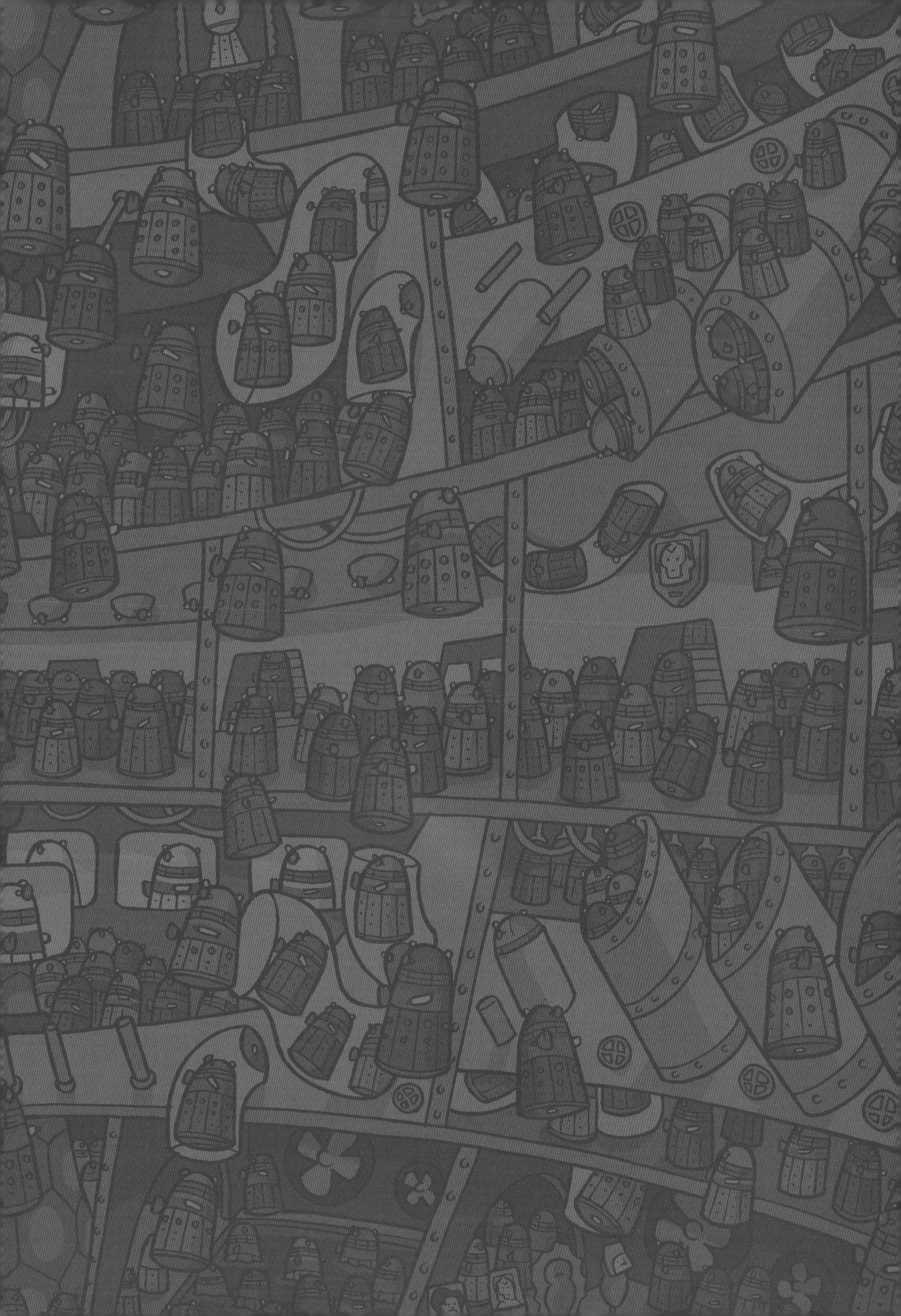

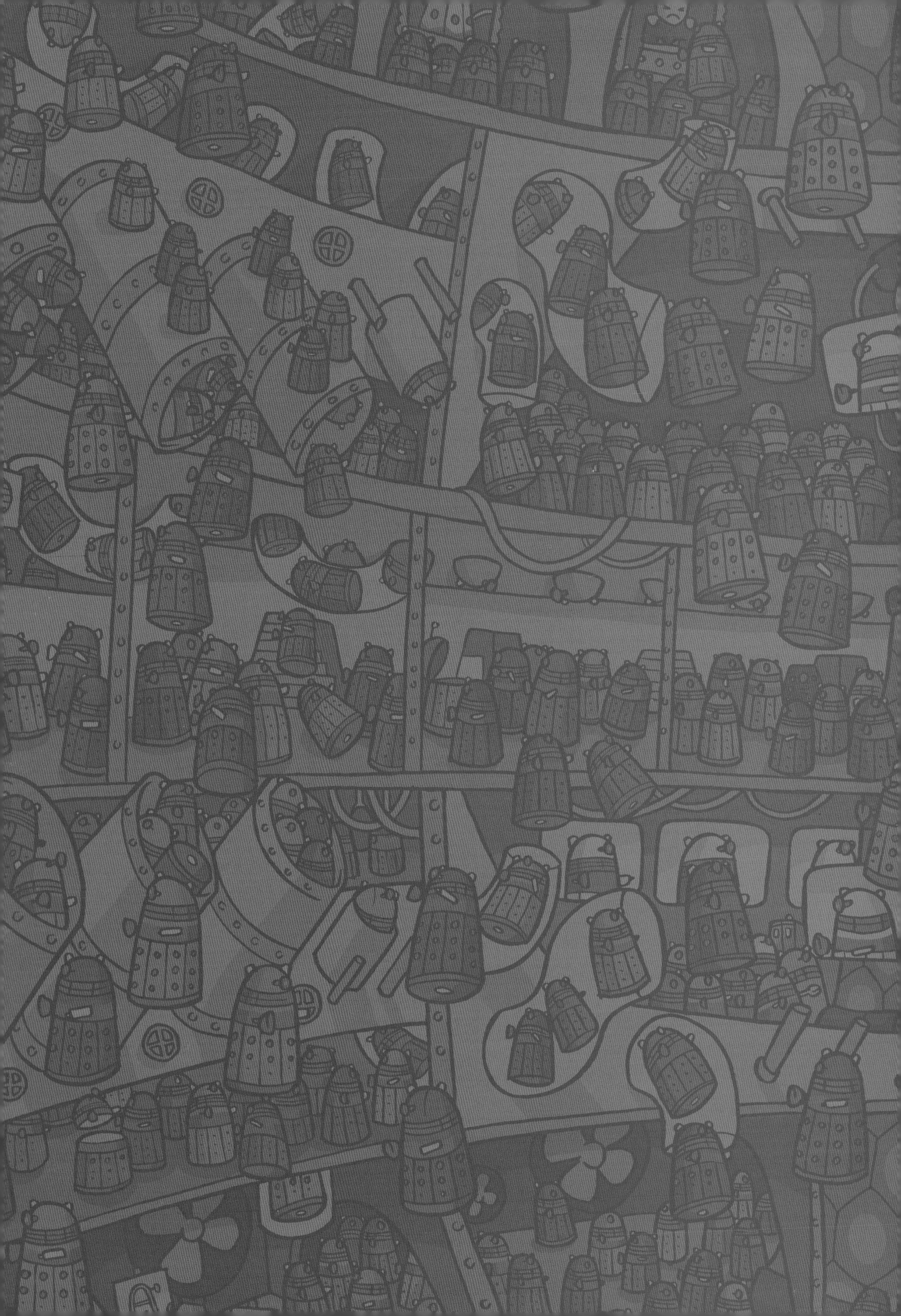